MOON OF BATTLE

By
J. J. ALLERTON

I0541456

ARMCHAIR FICTION
PO Box 4369, Medford, Oregon   97501-0168

A PLANET WHERE PEACE SEEMED IMPOSSIBLE

Driving a gas truck down highway 63 was one thing, but Pratt Marsh discovered that driving it across the mountains and wastelands of the moon was another, especially when it was millions of years in the future!

He found midgets, stone-men and giants, all with various levels of mental powers ranging from telepathy to stupidity. These were some of the curious inhabitants of Luona.

But it seemed to Pratt that this world had been created for just one purpose: deadly, bloody war. Conflict overwhelmed everyone who set foot on its ravaged surface. Could a simple earthman survive on this planet of eternal struggle?

FOR A COMPLETE SECOND NOVEL, TURN TO PAGE 119

CAST OF CHARACTERS

PRATT MARSH
It was all new to him, the gravity, the customs—but the way everyone wanted to battle with him was infuriating!

MOGLU
A race of giants that looked Cro-Magnon yet they were one of the more intelligent Luonar species—could they be trusted?

LAERI
Not lacking in courage, he believed in fighting for family and for friends—possibly at the cost of his own life.

JANNSI
With huge bald heads, these midgets were experts in the art of hypnotism. What insidious plan did they have for Luona?

AT-TU
Any outsiders that crossed his path generally died. So what was the mysterious bargain he had made with the Hammars?

MAERI
The customs of her people were very clear, once Pratt saved her life, she belonged to him…

CHAPTER ONE

'OLD BALDY' showed his dun-colored top, twenty miles ahead. And in between, was the barren desert, with only a cactus rearing its twisted, melancholy shape to relieve the monotony of flatness. The narrow ribbon of highway was a straight line, one end of which was his truck and the other, Old Baldy.

Theodore Pratt Marsh hummed a tuneless, cheerless air. And hunched closer over the wheel. Totomachi's hairpin turns and sudden, breath-taking dips took all the skill and strength of his arms to negotiate. Then he was over the last rise and was sweeping down into the last turn.

Pratt Marsh was thankful for the full moon, this night. This last curve was almost a right-angled one. And the long trailer body had to be swung over far to the left, in order to safely make the grade. He braked gently and shifted into third and felt the lever's free motion.

"...Cat's! Something's wrong!" he yelped, as the shifting lever rode free without meshing.

Sweat broke out on his forehead. And the night wind, cool and clean, turned the perspiration into the clammy feel of death's touch.

Pratt's eyes narrowed into piercing watchfulness. The slightest wrong move would send the truck careening over the sheer side of the mountain, to fall the half mile into the canyon below. And in the thirty-foot trailer behind him was thirty thousand gallons of high-test aviation gasoline. Too quick a turn would shift the liquid cargo and tip the truck.

And he was riding free!

He depressed the brake pedal gently. Already the trailer wheels had gathered enough momentum to make the whole business of braking, risky. And if he let the pedal down all the way, it would just burn out the brake lining. He let his foot come off it slightly, then pressed gently at it once more. He could feel the back end ride up hard. He caught sight of the speedometer. The needle was at the fifty-mark! And just ahead, a hundred yards, was the blind turn.

This was it. He had to let the truck come out past the center line just so far, then bring it in, and not too fast, either, toward the right. He was around the curve and almost where he was safe. And a car came *up* the grade at a speed far beyond the judicious, and too fast for maneuvering on the narrow, two lane highway.

Pratt's lips framed curses, even as his strong hands twisted savagely at the steering wheel. Behind him, the trailer answered the command of the wheel. He could almost feel the gas shifting in its steel envelope. And *did* feel the trailer tip! He rode the wheel desperately giving it all the right it would take, until the outside wheels were almost on the soft shoulder. The trailer tipped crazily right and left, then as he brought the truck to an even keel, the other car swept by.

His hands were wringing wet and were clamped so tight against the steering wheel, he loosened the fingers only with an effort. A deep sigh welled up from within him. The worst was now over. It was all down hill but with only a two percent grade. Then he was on the flat and riding smoothly once again.

He knew there was a filling station at the foot of Baldy. And a repair shop at the rear of the station. The truck was in gear and all he had to do was keep rolling.

The miles sped by. He had the road all to himself. Not another car was to be seen. He drove with one hand on the wheel and the other draped out the cab. The wind swept through the open window and cooled his warm skin. The desert was smooth with only the slightest undulations of sand formations. And the moonlight was as bright as sunlight. He passed a Saguaro cactus and saw that the shadow cast by the giant tree was as distinct as if the sun had cast it. He stuck his head out of the cab window and looked up.

The moon was a great silver ball riding against a deep blue backdrop. Never had he seen so great a moon. It seemed to fill the whole sky. Suddenly he blinked his eyes. And stepped hurriedly on the brake. The truck came to a smooth stop.

He blinked his eyes again. Something was wrong! He looked up at the moon again. And knew that his first glance had not been wrong. The moon was growing in size! But that was impossible...unless the moon was coming closer.

Pratt's mouth opened in a grotesque grimace...and froze that way. Not only was the moon coming closer but the whole landscape was acting as though he was on a ship in a heaving sea. The desert swam before his eyes...the moon kept getting larger...*larger...larger!*

Then something gripped his senses, a vast pressure took hold of his midsection and made him double up in horrible, excruciating pain. And an invisible hammer struck him across the back of his head. Blackness enveloped him.

CHAPTER TWO

PRATT opened his eyes and felt nausea grip him. Hurriedly, he opened the cab door...and flew out. *Literally flew!* He went skidding a good ten feet, gathering a mouthful of fine sand as he did so.

He lay face down for several seconds until he felt he could safely arise. Then with a single movement he came to his feet ... and went sailing twenty feet straight up into the air. He landed on straddling legs. And remained rooted to the spot on which he stood. A sickly, silly grin spread over his mouth. He had landed, facing the truck. With infinite caution be made his way to the truck, sliding one foot past the other in a shuffling slow motion dance. Slowly, he lowered himself to the running board and sat there, looking about him in amazement.

Above him in the dark blue sky blazed a gigantic ball. He peered intently at it. It couldn't be! Yet there seemed to be the visible proof of it. That large ball floating so serenely in the sky above was the Earth. He could see the dim outlines of two continents on the surface in view, North and South America.

He sat there, too stunned to move. What and how had it happened? *Where* was he?

He got to his feet again. And holding to the sides of the cab, he moved around to the front of the truck. There, he leaned against the radiator and looked about him.

The truck was parked on some sort of a highway. At least it was smoother than the ground immediately to the right and left of the truck. The road led straight ahead until it disappeared into the horizon. Pratt was quick to note the flatness of the surrounding countryside.

A speculative look came into his eyes and the strong tanned brow knit in thought.

"Now," he thought, "I don't know *how* I got here. But I'm reasonably sure of *where* I am. Unless the other planets have continents like those two I'm looking at. And I don't think so. So this is the moon! And to bear my theory out, the thinness of the air and the lack of gravity should be proof enough.

"Okay then. I'm on the moon. Me and a gas wagon loaded with thirty thousand gallons of high test. Now what?"

The last had been wrung from him as a strange, and confusing sound came to him. At first he thought it was the sound of a loon. Then as the sound came closer, he thought it was the high whine of an airplane motor.

It proved to be neither. Nor was it anything he was familiar with. Rolling toward him in the bright earth light, were a half-dozen strange creatures. They rolled up to within a few yards of the parked truck and stopped there. Then, to his amazement, the odd creatures straightened up and revealed themselves to be men. Or at least something which resembled men. There was a distinct and notable difference. They had four arms, two of which came from their shoulders and the other two jutted from that part of their bodies just above the waist.

"Who are you?"

The words came to his ears. He looked about him. And heard again!

"Who are you?"

It was then he realized that these strange beings were speaking to him. Yet not speaking. For he didn't see them open their mouths.

"Thought waves. Answer!"

THEN HE got it. They didn't speak. They merely thought the questions. And somehow they were transmitted to him. He realized at the same instant that since such was the case, he had better control his thoughts. At least until he found out whether or not they were friendly.

Some sixth sense made him look closely at the group. There had been six of them. Now there were only four. And turning, he spied the other two rolling toward him from two directions. They were only a few feet off when he saw them. Then they were erect and on him. He only had time to glimpse a pair of the cruelest looking faces he had ever seen. Then he was thirty feet in the air in a gigantic leap which took him out of their path and far to one side. He saw them peer about in bewilderment. And heard the others think:

"There, fools! Over there."

And anger took hold of him. What right had they to attack him? He had given them no reason to.

"Okay, damn you," he whispered softly. "If it's a fight you want…"

Then he jumped again. He had seen that they were unarmed. And no one had ever denied Pratt Marsh lacked courage. In fact he was a little on the foolhardy side.

His leap almost put him on top of one of the moonmen. His fist lashed out and caught one of them on the side of the neck. A look of awe came into Pratt's face at the handiwork of the blow. There had been a sharp, cracking sound and the one he hit left his feet in a great arching flight, to land ten feet away in a heap. Nor did it take more than one look to show Pratt that his blow had killed the stranger.

The other had turned at the same instant and wrapped his four arms around Pratt's middle. At the same time, the others, who had been waiting for just that to happen, doubled themselves up and came rolling forward to help.

Pratt twisted savagely about and went spinning around like a human top. The moonman's body rose, as if by levitation, until it was practically horizontal. Then, as Pratt continued to whirl in ten-foot leaps, the moonman's body rose past the horizontal plane.

The moonman's face was only a few feet removed from Pratt's, and even as he went bounding about in his gravity defying leaps, Pratt had time to observe the other's face. Grey in color, the skin was flabby and fell in fleshy roll across the cheekbones, like the dewlaps of a bloodhound. The eyes, like a cat's, were all pupil, a mud colored brown. Then the other opened his mouth and Pratt drew back in horror. Slime-green teeth, each a sharp pointed bit of bone, protruded past the lips. And a fetid odor came from the parted lips.

It didn't take more than a few seconds. Pratt noticed that in spite of the fact the monster had four arms, their grip was rather weak. And when his terrific spin combined with centrifugal force, something had to give way. It was the moonman who did. Spread-eagled, he went shooting off to land with a skidding thud on the sand, directly in the path of his friends, rolling to his rescue.

WHIRLING, Pratt made for the truck in two immense jumps. Then he was in the cab and stepped on the starter. The motor caught with a muffled roar. He shifted, sub-con-sciously, before he remembered that the shifting lever was broken. His jaw went slack, as the mechanism meshed. And he was off in a cloud of dust.

He didn't know whether or not the hard packed surface he was riding on was a road. He only knew that it led away from these men who were obviously not friendly. The accelerator went clear to the floorboard as he gave it all the gas it would take. Then, when he had put distance between him and the four-armed men, he relaxed and permitted his foot a more normal pressure.

His face reflected unconcern and he whistled through his teeth in his usual, untuneful manner. But his mind was busy in thought:

"All right, now, T. Pratt Marsh, we've got to figure this out. The phenomena of the levitation is something which at the moment must remain a mystery.

"The facts are these. To wit: one, while driving on U. S. 63, I was overcome by a strange blackout. Two, on my recovery I find myself in strange surroundings, presumably the moon. And why the moon? Because, unless my eyes deceive me, yonder planet is the Earth. Three, the moon is inhabited. And four...what was that?"

Perplexity screwed his face into sour lines. The moon was inhabited all right. Another scream or sound similar to one had come to him. Again he braked the truck to a stop. His mind, occupied with the mystery of the present, was once more alert to his surroundings. And they differed from that which he had just left.

The flat, arid plain had given way to a rolling verdant terrain. The belt of sand he was riding was a tan colored waist a hundred yards wide, set between the green of the countryside. To his right was a small stand of trees similar in shape and size to the familiar poplar. He cocked an ear in their direction. The sound had seemed to come from there. He waited for a few seconds to hear if it would be repeated, then just as he started the motor again, it rose into the thin air. And it was human. More, Pratt could have sworn it was a woman's voice!

The sound came from the depths of the trees. Then there burst into view, a *woman,* running in his direction as fast as she could. And immediately behind her, was the most gigantic man Pratt had ever seen.

HE ACTED by instinct. In an instant he was out of the truck. Under the seat was his truck jack. And it had a handle that could prove to be a murderous weapon. The heavy steel rod felt good in the palm of his hand.

He stood for the barest second watching the chase: the woman, bare legs churning the grass and the lumbering giant behind her. Then he leaped forward in huge bounding steps to meet them.

He was still unaccustomed to the strange lack of gravity and over-jumped his mark. His last leap took him over the heads of the two. He looked downward at them as he past over their heads and saw that she was a beautiful—and well-formed girl. Then he was on the ground again and had turned to face the monstrous being. Behind him, he could hear the panting breaths of the girl.

He bent in a crouch and peered at the giant, trying to gauge the angle of attack. The giant waited for him, his huge body stooped, head bent forward and eyes showing an animal bewilderment at the strange arrival of Pratt. Pratt waited for the other to make the first move. But the giant was too befuddled to do other than stand and look at Pratt.

Pratt became a bit tired of the tableaux created by their wariness. Stepping toward the other in slow, mincing steps, he came to within a few feet of the giant. And the something that had been bothering him at the back of his mind came clear to him now. This huge being facing him was like an animal insofar as intelligence was concerned.

One look at the beetle-brow, forehead sloping back until the eyebrows and forehead met the dull, animal-look in the eyes, told him that insofar as initiative was concerned, Pratt would have to make the first move. And behind him he heard the girls warning as he stepped in:

"Careful! Moglu has the strength of ten men!"

"Right," Pratt thought. "And the brains of a fly."

Then they were a few feet apart and suddenly Pratt moved like lightning. He had remembered what had happened when he struck the first man he had met on the moon and he had an idea that his fist would carry enough power for what was needed here. The giant still regarded him with the same puzzled look as Putt moved in. Then, as the Earthman lashed out with his fist, the giant moved also. And with a speed that was amazing. One hand swept downward and caught Pratt's fist and the other circled his waist. And Pratt was lifted high in the air.

But Moglu only held the other close to him.

"No, my friend, not quite the brains of a fly," Moglu said softly.

Pratt's jaw dropped in surprise. And Moglu grinned broadly at the expression on his captive's face.

"And now, what?" the soft voice of the giant taunted Pratt.

Pratt twisted madly in the other's grip but to no avail. Moglu only grinned and the arm around Pratt's waist tightened in inexorable pressure. Then Pratt drew back his right leg and kicked downward as hard as he could. The kick caught Moglu squarely on the kneecap. Gone was the stolid look in the eyes of the giant. And gone was the blankness of the face. Instead the giant's features grimaced in sudden pain. And he released Pratt as though he was a hot coal.

Pratt landed lightly and before Moglu could recover from the kick, Pratt kicked him on the other knee. And Moglu began to dance in pain, howling as he did so. And every time he landed, Pratt would kick him, saying:

"Yeah! The brains of a fly!"

CHAPTER THREE

PRATT WAS beginning to enjoy himself. But his enjoyment didn't last long. Moglu had been hopping up and down, to land first on one leg, then the other. And as he had landed, Pratt had kicked. Suddenly Moglu jumped, just as Pratt kicked and Pratt sprawled flat on his back when the kick missed its mark.

Before he could move, Moglu had leaped on him. And this time the giant's arms gripped like the coils of a boa constrictor. Pratt had one hand free. The other was held close to his side by Moglu's encircling grip. Pratt new it would only be a matter of seconds before the giant's grip would crush the breath and life from his body. And with only one hand free there wasn't much he could do.

His breath whistled from between his lips in a thin piping whistle. His chest felt as if an unbearable weight was pressing him into the earth. Slowly, as if in slow motion, Pratt brought his free hand up and fastened it into the shaggy beard of the face above him. And with his last remaining strength, he pulled Moglu close—and bit as hard as he could into the broad, fleshy nose, close to his own.

Once again, Moglu howled in pain. And released for a second the pressure of his grip. It was enough. Pratt wriggled free, and rolling swiftly to one side, managed to get to his feet before the other recovered.

But Pratt hadn't taken one thing into consideration. The distance he had rolled. When arose he saw that he was a good ten yards from Moglu. And although it took only a few seconds to get back, the giant had also regained his feet. Now they were as it was in the beginning.

Pratt was panting slightly, not only from his efforts but also from the effects of the lighter atmosphere. Moglu watched his approach with decided misgivings. Pratt's mind was no longer an open book. And he did not fight according to rules.

Pratt began a circling movement. To him it was at an ordinary pace, but to the giant, Pratt was a whirling human top. No matter how fast Moglu moved to face the Earthman, he never quite succeeded. So that when Pratt leaped at last, Moglu had his hack to him. And this time Pratt had a greater advantage than before.

Moglu's confidence had vanished.

Pratt landed full on the other's back. And while he encircled the giant with one hand, he held the other free. Then, disregarding Moglu's vicious maneuverings to displace him, Pratt swung several vicious blows to the shaggily bearded face. At first they seemed to have no effect. But as the iron-hard fist continued to land with monotonous regularity on the same spot, the sum total of the blows finally beat Moglu.

Pratt felt the giant shudder, then with a suddenness that was startling, Moglu fell to the ground.

There was squealing sound from behind him and Pratt whipped around to face the new danger. And found his neck encircled by a pair of soft warm arms. And felt a pair of soft warm lips pressed against his. He drew back in sheer surprise. But as the girl continued to kiss him, he answered the caress. When at last they drew apart, Pratt had to admit it was the warmest reception he had had so far; and the most welcome.

He regarded the lovely, young face only a few inches from his and found himself comparing it with those he had known upon Earth. The Kates, Janes, Sallys and the rest he had known suffered by comparison. Suddenly she pouted.

"So you have kissed others," she said. Then she withdrew from his arms.

HE GAVE himself a mental kick. She had read his mind. But before he could answer, he became aware of another presence. Turning swiftly, he saw that Moglu had regained consciousness and was approaching.

Pratt was beginning to weary of this constant battling he had to do. Of course he knew that all he had to do was get back to the truck. But that would only leave the girl to her fate. And for all he knew, it might be one worse than death.

To Pratt's surprise, Moglu, when he had approached to within a few yards of the Earthman, went to his knees. And crawled the rest of the distance that way. When he arrived almost at Pratt's feet, he lifted his head and said:

"Do as you wish, mighty warrior. I am yours."

Pratt's mouth opened in surprise. Now what? Nor was the situation made any clearer when the girl also dropped to her knees and made the same announcement.

"Hey!" he yelped at this sudden strange turn in affairs. "What goes here?"

The two on their knees looked up at him in open-mouthed surprise. It was Moglu who answered:

"Why, it is quite simple. We are yours, as a sort of prize for your feat of arms in conquering me. And you must consider us your slaves."

"Now—wait—a—minute," Pratt drawled.

"...Really," Moglu continued. "You should not let your feelings, that is, your moral disinclination to accept the situation, interfere with the *status quo*. It has been all too apparent to us that you are a visitor from another world. As such we are deeply interested in you. But because we must behave in the manner that is the rule for our individual races, your reception at my hands could not have been any different than it was. However, it has all turned out for the best, since you succeeded in overpowering me. And speaking for myself, I am thankful that such is the case."

A pained expression came into Pratt's face. This—this Pithecanthropus Erectus, this atavism who would have fetched a top price at any Odditorium on Earth, to speak as he did was beyond Pratt's power to believe. It just couldn't be!

Moglu, tiring of his position and seeing that Pratt didn't seem to know what to do, took matters into his own hands. Arising, he started off in the direction of the gas truck. The girl also arose and followed him. Pratt, seeing that matters were getting a little out of hand, also started for the truck.

He lagged behind, purposely, first to gather his strayed wits; and to reason out what to do when they were all at the truck.

"Very interesting," Moglu was saying, as Pratt arrived. "Of course, you realize that all this is a mystery to us. Our knowledge of anything mechanical is at the best, superficial. And confined to the most simple of objects, such as the wheel and water clock. However, I can admire what is all too apparent in this vehicle's construction."

"Okay, professor," Pratt said sharply. "I'll take it from here."

"Splendid!" Moglu said benignly. "We await your tale with what can best be described as bated breath."

Pratt gave Moglu a sour look. And began:

"Only a short a time ago, I was driving on a desert highway on that planet." He pointed to the Earth. "Something happened and I find that I have been transplanted, truck and all, to the moon. Now, it's obvious that some force or power, operating from the moon..."

"Wait!" Moglu halted the tale.

PRATT'S glance should have shriveled the ten-foot giant down to Pratt's size. But it only glanced off the dull, stupid looking countenance, as water from the rocks. If anything, Moglu bore a more animal looking appearance than ever.

"If you hold to the theory that the force which brought you here was man made, I can assure you that it is an erroneous conjecture." Moglu said. There was a trace of condescension in his manner. "Although our scientists have the *latent* mental ability to perhaps, and I say, perhaps, with a good deal of mental reservation, seeing that their pre-occupation with the problems which..."

"Shut up!"

The girl, who had been following Moglu's words with an air of profound admiration, shrank back in alarm at Pratt's sudden, explosive command. As for Moglu, his eyebrows disappeared completely within the depths of the hair that started at his eyebrows.

"Shut up!" Pratt stormed in irritation. "And listen to me! First of all, who are you? And let the girl talk," he hastily said as he saw Moglu open his mouth.

"Why—" she hesitated. "I am Maeri."

"Well, go on," he prompted, when she paused after telling her name. "Tell me more. Where do you come from? Who are your people? Whom do I see about getting back?" The last, he realized, was a foolish query.

To his amazement, she burst into tears. Instinctively, he stepped forward and placed his arms about her shoulders. She nestled close into them. But the tears continued unabated.

"Now, listen," he said gently. "I didn't mean anything, that is, I..."

"Do you mind, Master," Moglu interjected softly.

Pratt turned and saw that the giant was smiling. And despite the prognathus cast to the jaw, the smile had a winning and gentle quality to it. Pratt nodded. But his arms remained close about the girl.

"I should have explained your situation," Moglu said. "After all, I realized from the very beginning that you were at a loss and the time would come when things would have to be cleared up for you. To come down to fundamentals. You and the vehicle you came in are now a permanent part, shall we say, of our life. It is obvious that you cannot return, since the how of your coming was due to an inexplicable, natural causation.

"This is the planet, Luona. You term it, the moon. I am Moglu, the highest form of mental life on Luona. The girl is Maeri, one of the tribe of Lamats, who are the most prevalent type of people to be found on our planet. She is the daughter of the chief of the Stamat division of the Lamats. Now, as to our acquaintance with the language you speak..."

Pratt had shown surprise, just then. Moglu had obviously read his mind.

"...Actually," Moglu continued, "our language is universal. That is, all the people speak the same tongue. I can only surmise that your ability to speak it stems from some unexplained but natural reason. So with our power of reading thoughts. We all have that power. But only to a limited degree. But of that, later. I imagine that the important thing now, is to find out what your plans are. Just what are they?"

CHAPTER FOUR

THE QUESTION, so bluntly asked, caught Pratt flatfooted. What were his plans? He sat on the running board. Maeri sat beside him, looking up into his features with a glance which so much as said, but of course you will get us out of this predicament.

Silence fell between them. The Earth had disappeared from view and a faint rosiness on the horizon heralded the break of a new day. The silence lengthened interminably. It was Moglu who broke it.

"The day is breaking," he said. "And we are not in friendly country. The city of the Stamats lies only a hundred mons* away. It is my suggestion that we go there. Efredi, Maeri's father, will make you welcome, for one thing. Ana another, because of the circumstances, you will be enabled to maintain a residence in Stamat."

Pratt understood what Moglu was driving at. He had rescued the girl, from what, he was still in the dark about. Or how it had come to be that she was being pursued. But he was sure that the giant would explain in due time. What was important, was as Moglu had said, they were in enemy territory and they had better scram from there.

He looked at the cab, reflectively. Moglu's immense bulk would never fit into its confines. But he could sit on the

*mon—a distance on Luona corresponding to an Earth mile.

trailer tank, directly behind the cab, in such a way that his feet would rest upon the connecting rod. Then if Pratt lowered the rear mirror, they could talk.

Maeri watched, wide-eyed and wondering, Pratt's every move. The truck started jerkily and she held back a squeal of terror at the sudden movement. But as they began a smooth rolling down the hard packed sand, and nothing untoward happened, she became more at ease.

And Pratt became more uncomfortable.

He had noticed her state of undress. But at the time he had been busily engaged in other matters. Now her proximity was a matter of discomfort to him. He wondered if all the girls on Luona dressed in as little clothes as she. He gave her a second, hurried glance and turned quickly away. She was dressed in a sort of sarong that extended to her waist. Another bit of cloth only partly concealed the budding womanhood. Her skin was warm looking and brown in color.

He looked once again into her face and found her eyes, two pools of hazel light, regarding him quizzically.

"You—like Maeri?"

"Um. Well...yes, I do."

Above them there was the sound of an ill-restrained chuckle. Moglu was finding the conversation amusing.

"That is well," she said. "We have many customs, here, which will be foreign to you. Because of what happened, I am more than just a prize. I am..."

"Hold it!" Pratt hastily said. "We'll settle that when we see your father."

She shrugged her shoulders. After all, it wasn't going to make much difference whom they saw. The rules of Luona had to be observed.

"Turn right, here," the voice of the giant directed, as they entered a wooded area.

PRATT saw then that there was a fork in the road. He did as directed and found after riding for a few minutes that the forest was thinning out. Already, the sun was fairly high in the sky and the light showed Pratt that they were in a rolling, hilly land, rich in grass and flowers. Then they were out of the forest and approaching the crest of a hill, higher than most of the others. The truck nosed over the top.

And Pratt's foot stepped hard on the brake.

The girl gasped and shrank against his shoulder. Pratt could only stare, wide-eyed and rather curiously at what had confronted them. It was Moglu who both recognized their danger and gave the command to turn:

"Ekfoos!" his voice rumbled in warning. "Reverse the vehicle! Quick! Ah..."

But Pratt was too engrossed in the approaching wave of mounted men, to pay more than a superficial heed to Moglu's warning.

At first he thought they were Arabs. The resemblance to the camel-mounted Bedouins was startling. Then he saw that what he took to be camels, were strange two-legged beasts. But in other respects the men were similar. Even in their dress, which consisted of an all-enveloping robe, like the Arab burnoose. And as they came close enough to be recognized, he saw that in their facial delineaments, the Arab and these were brothers.

Not until the first wave of mounted men were almost on them, did Pratt realize that these men intended harm. Then he saw bared swords, scimitar shaped, flashing in the sunlight. And knew from the wild shouts and features alive in the light of the approaching battle that their mission was not of peace.

"Lay flat on the top," he shouted to Moglu. Then shoving the girl to the floor, he put the truck into gear.

And drove directly into the first wave of mounted men!

Whatever their expectations, they certainly didn't expect him to do what he did. The truck plowed through them like a bowling ball coming in for a pocket hit. Animals screamed in pain. The men's faces contorted in fear and anger, as they fell from their mounts. They had almost won through the last wave, when the truck's motor went out with a stuttering sound.

Pratt pounded frantically at the starter. There was a grinding, coughing sound from the truck's innards. But that was all.

Savage faces peered into the cab. Savage voices spit expletives at the terrified occupants. There were shouts, exultant, excited, from behind, somewhere. Pratt heard Moglu give voice to his bull-like bellow of rage. Then there came the sound of a scuffle and a thud, as of some heavy body falling to the sand.

There was the sudden commanding shout of a voice from the window at the girl's side and a new face appeared at the window. Smoldering brown eyes, savage in lust, peered in at them. A nose, curving as the scimitar blade, dominated the cruel face. Lean-fleshed, talon fingers reached in and pulled at the girl. And Pratt went berserk!

DESPITE THE narrow confines of the cab, he lashed out in a vicious straight arm at the sneering visage. The blow caught the man high on the cheekbone and parted the skin as neatly as though Pratt's fist was a surgeon's scalpel. The blow also sent the other spinning from the truck as if he'd been hit by a pile driver.

Voicing incoherent threats, Pratt leaped from the truck and disregarding the swords and the overpowering difference in numbers, charged in headlong attack. He was a whirling cyclone and almost as savage and damaging. Ekfoos went spinning away from the pounding fists and kicking feet as though they had been caught up in the path of a whirlwind. Pratt knew only this.

That he was a peace loving man. And ever since his arrival on the moon, he had been at almost continuous struggle against someone. First, the weird men whose locomotion was to roll like a child's hoop. Then Moglu. Now these! Well, he'd show them how an Earthman fights.

For a few seconds he was able to fight in close where his superior speed and agility were advantages they could not overcome. Then they became aware of that fact. And ran from him. To form a circle about him. A circle of steel! Their swords were like the bars of a cage against which he knew it was hopeless to rage.

Then, from the other side of the truck, there came the muted cry of the girl, her voice rising in protest and ending on a note of terror. Pratt took in the situation in a single glance. The nearest men were about ten feet removed. Their gloating looks showed their joy at what they thought would be his end. A carcass, spitted on the end of someone's blade.

Bending until he was almost double, Pratt started at a run for the group nearest the truck. He took short, quick steps. Then, when he was only a few feet away, he took a tremendous leap, clearing not only the men but the truck as well.

He saw then, when he landed on the other side what had made Maeri cry out as she did. A burnoosed savage held her in his grip. She was bent almost double and he was tearing at her upper garment. And surrounding them were a dozen men, laughing aloud at her predicament, pounding each other's shoulders at the spectacle.

In a single bound, he was at their side and his fist had landed with bone crushing force against her attacker's jaw. The man left his feet and flew into some of those watching, sending them to the ground also. Pratt noticed that he did not arise with the rest. The girl sank to the ground, shielding her half-naked body with trembling fingers. He stood over her straddle-legged and waited the onslaught of the Ekfoos. He knew it was a hopeless situation. There were hundreds of them. Already, the thirty or forty men he had seen were augmented by several times that number, in just a few seconds.

Maeri looked up at the snarling, unafraid face above her and was filled with a queer, sudden feeling that all would turn out well. Such courage could not go unrewarded. Then she thought of the laws of Luona and felt a natural fear for him. It was kill or be killed in such a situation. That was the law!

Savage-eyed and unafraid, Pratt faced them. His mind told him that there was no way out. And he saw from their looks that it was so. Now they were coming in for the kill. Voices from the outskirts of the mob warned those nearest to watch for his leaps—watch that they did not come too close!

And a bull-bellow boomed:

"Alive! I want that man alive!"

THE MOB parted and a man stepped forward. One look at the way his arrival was greeted and Pratt knew he was the leader of the Ekfoos. And justly so by his appearance alone. A full seven feet high, his magnificent figure was robed in a burnoose of rainbow hue. A naked blade was thrust through the belt of his robe. He advanced until he and Pratt were only a yard apart.

Pratt's eyes narrowed in speculation at the close view of the man. Power, determination, cruelty were writ large on this man's countenance. And more. For in the dark, narrow-set eyes was to be seen intelligence also.

The thin slash of his mouth tightened into even crueler lines, as he saw the girl.

"What have we here?" he asked.

Pratt straightened from the fighting crouch he had assumed and answered in biting terms:

"What was the idea of all this? Where do you get the idea that you can attack people...that you..."

"Who are you? And who is this girl?" hawk-face asked, breaking into Pratt's diatribe.

"My name is Theodore Pratt Marsh. And this girl is Maeri, daughter of the chief of Stamats. But that's neither here nor there. I want..."

"Enough! No one asks anything of At-tu!" He gave the truck a close look of inspection, walking around it and coming back to Pratt after he was through, continued:

"What is this thing? How does it go?"

Pratt bit his lips in vexation. There was no doubt that the truck was to these people as the phonograph was to the first natives to see it in darkest Africa, a thing of black magic. And a thought came to him. If it worked...

"This," Pratt began, his voice taking on a rich, fruity tone, "is the chariot which brought me from another world."

At-tu was puzzled.

"Chariot? Another world? You speak in riddles. Wait...I know! It is the work of the Hammars! You are their emissary. Take him, men... Alive!"

And before the stunned Pratt could do more than lift his hands in futile defense, he was overwhelmed. Twenty bodies bore him to the ground. Fists lashed at him. Fingers tore at him. All his struggling was unavailing. From somewhere in the voluminous robes, they brought forth rope, with which they bound him.

He lay on the ground and looked his defiance at At-tu. At-tu paid not the slightest heed to him. Stepping to the girl who had been at the bottom of the heap and had been knocked unconscious by a blow, he pulled at her hair, bringing her face, pale in its stunned coma, to a close view.

"Hmm…daughter of Komu. She'll bring a fancy price. That is if I decide to return her. Toat!"

A villainous looking man appeared from the farthest edge of the crowd gathered around the two. Shifty eyes blinked up at At-tu. A flaccid mouth twisted in twitching words:

"Aye, Master?"

"Have these carrion brought to my city. And see to it the man does not escape. Give the girl to the women in my compound. And say, that she must be made ready for my return."

"Aye, Master! Here knaves," he shouted to some of the men.

Four of them stepped forward and lifted Pratt and the girl to two of the strange animals. Then they bound them to the saddle-like arrangement on the animals' rump. And after Toat and the four he had designated had mounted, they made off in the same direction from which they'd come.

At-tu watched their departure with brooding eyes. But he had already forgotten them. He had more important things on his mind. The conquest of Luona!

PRATT HAD begun to wonder how long this ride was going to last. Long ago, his flesh had chafed where the rope or whatever it was that held him prisoner, had bit into his skin. Now, every jolting stride of the animal's gait made him grit his teeth and clench his lips to prevent him from crying aloud. Toat, riding alongside watched him with gleeful relish. And every now and then voiced a gibe:

"So…how does it feel, dog of a Hammar? Soon, you'll know a greater agony. Keep a stiff lip. The hero a craven will be soon as the tipped lash strikes—for the hundredth time."

Pratt grinned in spite of his pain. He recognized Toat for what he was, a jackal, trailing the lion, knowing after the feast there would be something for him. But in Pratt's heart there was the growing conviction that the fire was going to be hotter than the frying pan. If it weren't for the girl... But it was too late for recriminations and hopeless to speculate on what the future held.

Maeri rode just ahead of Toat and Pratt. She had regained consciousness just after they had started off. Not by a single sign had she shown her awareness of Pratt, directly behind her. She seemed steeped in a misery too great for her to be interested in anyone else's. Either that, or indifferent to their fate.

Their mounts rode free, without halter. And at terrific speed. Pratt gave his a thorough inspection. More like a bird than anything else, it had a head that was devoid of hair. A neck, long and muscular made Pratt think of an ostrich. But the hooves were cloven and there were no wings.

Then, just when the flesh could no longer bear the agony of chafing, the ride ended. They had ridden up the crest of a hill and before them stretched the city of At-tu.

Their mounts stood still on the hilltop. And in that interval of stillness, Pratt took in the situation. He had expected something different from what he saw. A city to him, was a collection of stone or brick homes. This, however, was a city of tents. Great, rainbow-striped affairs, they stretched across the whole width of the valley in which the city was laid.

Whoever had planned the city had done so with an eye for its defense. On three sides it was surrounded by sheer-walled escarpments. The only entrance, as far as Pratt could see, was down the gentle slope of this hill they were on. Despite his predicament, he found it in him to admire what he saw. Yet he could not understand why, after making certain that the city was impregnable to assault on three sides, the fourth was left open in this manner.

His muscles contracted in painful reminder of his condition and he flexed them in a sudden, strong move. And felt the bonds give slightly. His face became a blank mask of flesh. Only his eyes showed the inner excitement he felt. He railed at himself for not having tested the strength of the ropes, before. Now it was too late. For Toat and the others had begun the descent of the hill.

CHAPTER FIVE

PRATT'S MOUNT moved with a dainty, careful, high-stepping manner. As if it were walking on ground carpeted with eggs. Pratt turned and observed the rest and saw that their mounts were also moving in the same manner. Then he realized in a sudden flash of inborn knowledge, the reason for it. Although it was hidden from human eyes, and perhaps only found through the animal sense of these strange creatures, they were moving on an invisible path.

The ground looked alike, everywhere. Then, one of the two-legged beasts stumbled. It was for the barest second, but in that second, the animal stepped off the path. And sank up to its fetlocks in the ground. Its mouth opened but no sound came from the distended throat. The rider, his face contorted in horror, leaped from the animal's back. And sank, also into the ground. If the animal was dumb, the human was not. Unutterable agony limmed the features. His lips contorted into the most awful expression of pain, Pratt had ever seen. While from the man's throat came shrieks of pure agony.

Slowly, the man and beast sank into the ground. And to Pratt's nostrils came the unmistakable odor of burning flesh. Louder and louder grew the man's shrieks as he sank lower into the mire of hidden flames. Steam arose from around the close held bodies. Pratt felt the cold sweat break over him. He looked around him and saw that, although the others were also aware of what had happened, not one made any move to rescue the man.

The man was now up to his hips in the ground. And he no longer shrieked as before. His voice had dwindled to a whimpering, animal sound. Then Pratt saw the man's eyes roll upward, horribly and he gave voice to a single, last shriek of despair. And was silent, forever.

Yet Pratt found that he was more horrified at the beast's agony than he was at the man's. For it was evident that the beast was dumb. And could only show his agony through his eyes. Pratt knew that the sight of the dumb animal's dying struggles would remain with him forever. He looked back once more, just as they reached level ground, but all that met his eye was the hummocks and humped grass.

Just before they reached the first line of tents which lay in a great circle of cleared land, they came to a moat about a hundred feet across. A narrow, wooden bridge was the only means of crossing the moat. Just beyond the moat, the first row of gaily colored tents stood. They rode across the bridge in single file.

At first sound of their mount's hooves on the wood, a great crowd of people came pouring forth from the tents in the immediate vicinity. And when they saw that two of the animals bore captives, shrieks of joy came from the throats of the assembled watchers.

Pratt saw that most of the crowd were women. But never had he seen such savagery as was displayed on the countenances of these women. Four of the guards moved in to surround the girl, as they rode in among the crowd. But Pratt was permitted to ride unescorted. It was not until they were well into the crowd of women and children, that he realized why they had formed a cordon about the girl.

THE GUARDS had drawn their sabers. But the crowd leaped forward in the face of the weapons and tried to reach the girl. The guards beat at them with the flat of their swords. But in spite of that, the crowd seemed intent on getting to the girl and from what he saw, tear her to pieces. Then they saw Pratt. And saw, too, that he was unprotected.

Their savage, hateful faces shown with joy, as they ran to him. Toat reined his mount in behind Pratt and watched the crowd's approach with grinning mouth. Pratt braced himself for their onslaught.

Then they were on him. Taloned fingers tore at his clothes; claw-like fingers raked at the skin on face and hands. In a few seconds half the clothes he wore had been torn from his body. His face was a welter of scratches from the clawing fingers. And no matter how he twisted in vain effort to escape their clutches, some of them managed to get to him. He began to wonder how long this was going to keep up. For new arrivals came from every section of tents they passed. It was a gamut he had to go through.

But just when he thought that surely this was the end, Toat shouted for them to, "go back to their cooking and whelps. This is At-tu's prisoner."

Pratt's head hung in weariness. His body ached intolerably. It seemed that every nerve, muscle and bone had been torn from its mooring.. He was only barely aware that they had reached their goal. He lifted his head and saw that they had paused before the largest tent he had ever seen. Fully two stories high, it stretched for a good twenty yards in diameter.

Maeri was lifted from her mount and carried into the tent. Then after a moment, the men came out and mounting again, rode down the narrow passage that was the street between the rows of tents. This time their journey was short. They came to an open space on which had been placed a wooden enclosure.

Toat rapped with the hilt of his sword at the gate that barred entrance. It swung wide and Pratt and Toat rode within. The gate swung shut behind them. Pratt looked about him with dazed eyes. He saw a half dozen of the now familiar tents, placed in such a way that they were several yards removed from the high, wooden fence. Armed guards patrolled the areaway between the tents. And were stationed also at regular intervals all along the wooden barrier.

"What have we here?" a thin, high-pitched voice cackled.

"Meat—for the pot," Toat answered. The words were meaningless…to Pratt. But the old man who had let them in went into a fit of laughter at the words, laughter in which Toat joined. Then he turned and rode through the gate.

"Ho, guards!" the old man cried.

Two of them came running at the command.

"Number three tent," the old man said.

Pratt was lowered from his animal and set upon his feet. The guards cut his bonds. And he promptly fell to the ground. They looked at him in silence for a second, then one of them brought his foot back and booted Pratt in the aide. He tried to roll from the kick but his muscles refused to answer to the mind's command. Once again the guard kicked. But Pratt only lay supine under the kicks. The other joined in the sport.

"Let them," Pratt thought. "It's as good a way to die as any."

But the old man had other ideas.

"Enough," he cried. But his eyes gleamed in enjoyment at the rare sport he was watching. "Carry the dolt; else he dies before we have our use of him."

THEY LIFTED him, amidst uproarious laughter and carried him the few yards to the tent the old man had designated. They threw him in as if he were a sack of bones. Nor did they turn to see whether he was alive or dead.

For a long time Pratt lay quiet, not alone because he was husbanding his strength, but also because to move even in the slightest degree was agony. Gradually the pain passed. And with it his mind came out of the daze it had been in. His senses stirred and he became aware of his surroundings—and companions.

He had been aware, but dimly, that he was not alone in his prison. Now that his mind was clear he rolled over and sat up. Sunlight filtering through the tent-cloth showed him that the tent held two others beside himself. One was a giant similar in appearance to Moglu. The other was a young man about his own age. He had a lean, strong-boned face, hungry looking and savage-eyed. The mouth however was wry in its expression.

"The pot will be full, Moglu," the young man said.

The giant, his head thrown back, laughed long and hard at what the other had said. His laughter at end, he said:

"Aye. Meat is cheap in Luona." And burst into another laugh.

Pratt looked from one to another in perplexity. Their talk didn't make sense. But then nothing made sense on this planet. He was sure of one thing, however. That whatever they were laughing at was not good. And that he had better start doing something about it. He remembered that his bonds had felt loose when he had suddenly tensed his muscles. Perhaps...

He held his body loose; then put all his muscle against the tightly binding ropes. He felt them give slightly. Once more he strained to the full power of the flesh's enduring. And felt the rope part from about his arms and body. The young man gasped at Pratt's display of phenomenal strength. And even the giant looked his amazement.

Pratt stood up and shook himself free of the ropes. Then he walked over to the others and gripping each of their bonds between his fingers, tore them free. For a few seconds there was silence broken now and then by smothered gasps as the circulation was returned to almost nerveless muscles and flesh.

The Earthman watched them, sober-eyed. Then when he saw that they had regained the use of their members, he said:

"Think you can do anything besides talk now that you're free?"

The hard-eyed moonman flushed at the words.

"You have great strength and courage," he said grudgingly. "But it will take more than that to set us free of this trap."

Pratt squatted beside the two. He gave the tent a casual yet all-inclusive glance.

"It doesn't look too tough, the way I see it," he remarked.

The two moonmen went tense at his words. What did he mean?

"Look," Pratt explained. "I don't know what's beyond this enclosure. But all that's out there, is maybe six or seven men. Between the three of us—and the rest of the prisoners, we should be able to take care of them. It's already night. In a few minutes it'll be completely dark. At least enough for our purpose. Wait," he said as the young fellow started to interrupt. "Explanations can wait until we get out of here. If we don't they won't be necessary."

The other saw Pratt's point of view. He nodded soberly.

"As you say," he agreed. "Explanations can wait. More, if we go free, they won't be asked. And you will have earned my gratitude. One thing…you are a stranger here?"

"Yes."

"Then allow me to take the lead."

"Okay by me. Just one thing. There was a girl with me. If we get out, we've got to get to Maeri."

"Maeri!" the name burst from the young man's lips with the explosive force of a shot. "Is she here?"

PRATT WAS taken aback by the other's sudden action. The moonman had come erect and was standing over Pratt like a vengeful God. His anger was so intense, he was quivering with it.

"Yes," Pratt said slowly. "Do you know her?"

"My sister," the other said. "At-tu dared to profane her. I'll have his blood for it."

"You'll have to share it with me," Pratt said. And his eyes were hooded in sudden, implacable hate.

As one the two started toward the flap.

"Hold," Moglu said suddenly. The giant's brow was furrowed in concentration. Then the wrinkles smoothed out and he said:

"My brother has a message for his master. He has been left alone with the vehicle. He feigned death and after the Ekfoos departed ran off to hide. Now he wants to know how he can assist?"

Pratt smacked his palm with a clenched fist. Damn! If only Moglu knew how to drive. And the giant in the tent said:

"It is not so difficult. Merely think your instructions. He will follow them."

Pratt's eyes widened. Of course! He had forgotten their ability to sense telepathic messages.

"Wait for my instructions," his mind flashed the command.

The giant then arose and joined the other two at the tent flap. Pratt spread the cloth, cautiously. A lone warrior stood just beyond the shadow of the tent. His back was toward them. He leaned against the shaft of a long spear. His head was bent forward, cheek resting on the shaft end. There was no one else to be seen.

Pratt stole out of the tent with infinite caution. Like shadows, the other two came at his heels. They were but a few feet from the slumbering guard when some sixth sense awoke him. He acted with amazing speed. But as fast as he was, Pratt was faster. Before the other had half completed the turn in their direction, Pratt had leaped for him. And in that leap almost lost his life. For when the guard turned, he brought his spear into a position of accouchment. And the broad, gleaming head met Pratt's flying leap. To the two behind Pratt, it looked like the spear had passed completely through his body. Then they saw Pratt's arm come up and encircle the guard's throat. And saw the other clamp tight against the mouth of the guard.

There was the sharp, cracking sound of bone breaking and the guard went limp in Pratt's grasp. It was the only sound that had been made.

Pratt pulled the spear from his shirt. It had passed through without touching the flesh.

"All right, mister. You take it from here."

Maeri's brother looked hastily around. There was neither sound nor sight of living thing. To their right, the dark bulk of a half dozen tents loomed. To their left was an open area perhaps twenty yards across. And beyond that, the gate. He turned right.

CHAPTER SIX

THEY STOLE along the walls of the tents. When they reached the farthest one, Maeri's brother paused. The other two came close.

"Jama-at, my father's Hafa* was taken to this tent," he whispered. "And with him were five of the best warriors in Stamat. Even without weapons, they will avail against these carrion."

Pratt wanted to ask how come, with weapons, they were taken prisoner, but decided to hold his peace.

Maeri's brother parted the flap and whispered softly:

"Jama-at! It is I, Laeri."

Pratt heard the muffled sound of voices. Then five forms stole from the tent. He saw then that they were strong looking, big men, dressed exactly alike in leather shorts and shirts that covered their breasts. The biggest of them came close to Laeri and said:

"How did you affect your escape? I saw you and the Moglu bound."

Laeri explained in a few words. Jama-at clasped Pratt's hand in a tight squeeze and said:

"I am yours to command. Ask what you will."

"Are any of the others armed?" Pratt asked.

Jama-at shook his head.

"If we had been armed," Jama-at explained somewhat sadly, "there would not have been any of us left alive to take prisoner."

"Well," Pratt said to himself. "You ask a silly question and you get the right answer."

Jama-at turned to Laeri, then and said :

"I see you have a spear. A beginning anyway. Well, there are four more of us, I think, in the fourth tent. Who else is prisoner of At-tu's, I don't know, but whoever they are will be more than willing to risk escape than the pot."

*Hafa-Commander of Komu, the chief of the Stamat's forces.

Again the pot. Pratt noticed that the word had a sinister connotation. But what it was, was a mystery to him. He shrugged his shoulders and turned to the rest. They were silently looking toward the tent in which the rest of Jama-at's men were incarcerated. It was then Pratt noticed an odd feature of the tent in question. Where all the other tents had their opening toward them, this one either had no opening, or it was at the other end.

The Earth had risen above the horizon and was shedding a light upon them that was almost as bright as that of the sun. For an instant, he wondered what was taking place upon that distant planet which had been his home. Then, as Jama-at started toward the tent that was their goal, all thoughts of Earth and home were erased. Something told Pratt that all was not as serene as they imagined.

Between each tent was an areaway of about ten feet. They passed the first of the tents on their way to the one in which the rest of the men were, when they crossed the space between two tents. Before they could do more than stare open-mouthed at the men who swarmed out at them, half of them were stretched on the ground, either wounded or dead. But their surprise was only momentary.

Then they struck back, savagely, with all the inspired daring and strength of lost men.

Pratt was a ravaging avenger, scourging whoever came in his path, for the ignominies he had suffered at the hands of all who had attacked him since his arrival on the moon. He had learned to gauge and allow for, the difference in gravity. He no longer leaped in wild jumps, but moved swiftly and surely to his goal. And those incredibly swift movements played havoc with the slower moonmen. As if that wasn't enough, he struck blows too fast for them to parry, even with sword or spear.

ALONE, HE accounted for ten of them. But the odds were too great. The whole compound had been aroused by the cries, shrieks, groans and bellows of the guards. Pratt and those with him fought silently. Somehow, Jama-at, Laeri and Moglu had seized weapons. They stood in a sort of rough triangle, shoulder to shoulder. Pratt, because of his greater advantage in speed and strength, ranged the length of the battle area.

The spear that was his weapon was dyed red for half its length, red from the blood it had bathed in. Nor was he unscathed. There were more than just a few nicks in his skin. Luckily, they were all minor wounds. Not so lucky were those with whom he'd come in contact. Dead and dying strewed the ground.

Suddenly the gate opened and into the arena came charging a veritable horde of warriors. Pratt took a single look, then dashed to the side of his friends. Men fell before the mad onslaught of his spear, used now as a club, like ten pins on a strike hit.

Jama-at's eyes gleamed in wild delight as he came among them.

"Ho!" he cried in a great voice. "Mine eyes have seen the greatest of warriors, this night. Death will be sweet, at your side."

Laeri and Moglu were silent but their eyes showed their respect.

The knot of warriors before them broke at the sound of a shouted command:

"Hold!"

It was At-tu!

Roughly shouldering aside those who were nearest to Pratt, he faced the four, on his face a sour look. He looked at the four men, then looked aside at the carnage their arms had created. Once again he looked at them.

"It is luck, indeed, that there were not more of you. I would have come back to an emptied village. Bah! And these call themselves warriors!"

He kicked at one of those who was pressed close to him. The kick sent the man scurrying. Having vented his spleen, At-tu turned once again to Pratt and his new-found friends and said:

"Well, since you are free, I am saved the business of seeking you. This is the night of the feast of Ramad. Laeri—Jamat—Moglu—stranger of iron...your choice! Slavery—or the pot!"

The four who were prisoners looked at each other. Pratt, with a question on his lips, the others showing only resolve. Even the ape-like face of Moglu showed the same courage and determination as the rest.

Maeri's brother suddenly remembered that Pratt was a stranger to what had been asked of them. He turned and started to unfold the mystery, but stopped as Pratt said:

"It's all right, Laeri. I'll go along with the rest."

At-tu grinned, then. But there was little of humor in the lip's twisted movement.

"Good. Then there is no need to delay the ceremony. Some of you collect the rest of the prisoners." The last was said to his men who immediately followed his command.

IN A moment there were twenty odd men standing about the brightly-lit open space. There was much laughter and shouting among At-tu's followers. In the confusion and hubbub, Moglu managed to whisper to Pratt:

"Now! It's your only chance to reach my brother. None here can intercept the message. Tell him what you will. And if this thing between you can save us, summon him."

It was as if Pratt became two people then. One, a corporeal body moving with the rest toward the doom At-tu had decreed, the other commanding and directing Moglu, wherever he was, to his will.

"Can you hear me, Moglu?" his mind asked.

"Aye," came the silent answer.

"Where are you?"

"Within the little hut where you and the girl were sitting."

"Good! Now on the...wait a minute. How did you manage to get that bulk of yours into the cab?"

Pratt actually *felt* Moglu stutter:

"Why—er—I must admit it was a tight squeeze. But after a moment I saw that I was too large. So..."

"So?"

"So I tore a hole in the roof."

Pratt had to grin as he got a mental picture of Moglu, the upper part of his torso jutting from the torn roof-top, like a caricature of a Hansom cab driver.

"No matter," he said forgiving the trespass. "On the panel in front of you are several bits of metal, attached to a linked bit of chain. One of these bits of metal is sticking in the panel. Turn it to the right."

He waited until Moglu announced he had done so.

"Now, just below the bits of metal is a lever. Turn it to the right also. Do you hear a sort of purring sound? Good. That means the motor is on. On the floor beside your right foot are two pedals. If you press the one on the right the truck will begin to move. The deeper you press, the faster the truck will move. That pedal is the gauge by which you judge the speed at which you move. The wheel close to your belly is the steering apparatus. If you turn it to the left, the truck will go left. To the right, it will go right. That is all that I can tell you. The rest is up to God."

There was a silence for a short interval. Then Pratt remembered that Moglu knew everything...but where to go. And as if in answer came the thought from Moglu:

"Don't worry. I will get there as speedily as possible."

Pratt sent up a silent prayer that Moglu would not fail them. Somehow, he had a feeling of the deepest optimism. But when he regarded their surroundings and realized that they had arrived at their destination, his heart sank down into his boots.

SO GREAT had been his concentration in getting what he wanted across to Moglu, he had not been consciously aware of the passing of time and place. Now his senses stirred and awakened, brought into sharp focus by the strangeness of his surroundings.

The prisoners and their guards, followed by what appeared to be most of the populace, had arrived at a cleft in the hills behind the great encampment of tents. In effect it was a shallow valley, skirted by the steep-sided hills. Within this valley was a great, circular place, like a gigantic earthen well.

Drawn up before the great depression was a large body of armed and blood-lusting soldiery. Ranks of them, three deep, had formed into a funnel-like neck through which the prisoners had to pass. At the end of the funnel were drawn up a number of unarmed men, At-tu at their head.

Pratt, Laeri, Jama-at and Moglu were the first to reach At-tu and the others with him. As the last of the prisoners came before him, At-tu gave a signal to the soldiers who immediately pressed close to the prisoners, hemming them in to prevent any attempt at escape. Then At-tu lifted his arm as a signal for silence. The huge, laughing throng, vibrant with excitement, became still at the gesture.

"My people!" At-tu's voice was a stentorian command for their attention. "This is the night of Ramad! It has been the age-old custom that on this night all who have been taken prisoner shall have their choice: slavery or the pot! And to those who accept the challenge of the pot, freedom and sanctuary for those who escape."

Laeri, standing close beside Pratt grunted a soft:

"Choice! Never in the memory of men, has anyone escaped."

"...There, prisoners, is the pot. The means of escaping are of your own choice," At-tu said, speaking directly to them.

He stepped back and the men, whom Pratt had noticed were unarmed, stepped forward and began a mumbo jumbo chant. As they chanted, they first faced the depression then turned their eyes upward to the Earth. Every time they raised their heads upward, they intoned, "Ramad!"

Pratt followed their gaze and saw that tonight, at this time, the continent of Europe was to be seen. A cluster of pinpoint lights were to be seen on the upper west side of the continent. An instant's calculation told him those lights were the city of London.

London! That great, civilized city, two hundred thousand miles away, teeming with... Pratt shook himself free of the despondency that had seized him on seeing the presumed city. His eyes narrowed and his chin set in stubborn lines. Despite what Laeri had said, hope still rode strong in his breast. There was still Moglu. The unseen, hidden danger of the pot was a phantasm created to frighten them into panic, he thought.

The priests, finished with their unintelligible intonings, retired to the background. At-tu stepped back also. Then the soldiers pressed forward relentlessly, their bared spears and swords held close against the hindmost prisoners, compelling them to move forward against those in front. In this manner the front rank, Pratt and his friends, were forced to the very lip of the depression.

CHAPTER SEVEN

SOMEHOW, Pratt was maneuvered into being the first on the edge. The bright glow of the Earth showed him the pit they were facing, in all its immenseness. It was a circular affair, thirty feet across and about the same depth.

"The ladder!" At-tu called out. "Use it to descend."

Pratt saw then that a ladder had been affixed against the straight side of the pit. He turned and descended without an instant's hesitation. The others followed with as little hesitation as Pratt.

For some reason, which Pratt attributed to instinct, he did not venture beyond the wall of the pit. Laeri, Jama-at and Moglu moved in beside him. But some of the others, seeing that nothing had happened after they arrived on the floor of the pit, moved toward the center.

Then Pratt saw repeated the drama that had taken place when Toat and the others had brought him to the tented city. The ground, which looked so firm, was the same sort of quagmire that existed on the gentle slope. It also had the same qualities. The first to venture on the ground beyond the wall sank to his knees in the soft ground. And from about the flesh there arose a slender column of steam. The man shrieked once, a shriek that was echoed by the multitude gathered above. Their, however, was one of unholy joy. The pot had found its first victim.

Nor was he alone in finding the hidden morass. At least ten more had followed him onto the thin earth surface and like him, were floundering below the thin sheath of protecting earth.

Instinctively, Pratt pressed closer to the protection of the wall. His eyes could not take themselves away from the unavailing struggle of those men. Beyond the first stricken cry, none of the others uttered a sound. Yet it was all too apparent that courage was not going to be enough. Further, the single apparent means of escape had been removed, the instant the last of them had set foot in the pit. For when Pratt, searching desperately for an exit looked to where the ladder had been, he saw it was no longer there.

No wonder they called it the pot! The men were literally being boiled alive! A carnal odor arose from their half-hidden bodies.

"Look!" Laeri, cried.

They turned their faces as one, in the direction he was pointing. Not all of them had found the boiling pit below the surface. Two men were pressed close against the wall at the opposite end of the circular pit.

There was a means of getting across!

Pratt made an inventory of the group on their side of the pit. Twelve men were on the comparatively safe side. But in the final analysis, how safe were they? Pratt figuring desperately for the way out saw that if there was a way, it would have to be at the opposite end.

To get to the other end, however, they had to cross the hidden morass. He didn't have to be told that At-tu would not provide any means toward keeping them alive. It was going to be entirely up to them.

"Wait here!" Pratt commanded.

Sticking close to the wall, he began a cautious circling of their prison. Once his light step felt the earth give and he froze into stillness. But it was only a soft spot and just at that point. Beyond it was safety. He skipped lightly over the danger area. Not until he reached the others at the opposite end did he feel safe.

Pratt's tightly drawn features relaxed slightly, when he had time to survey the situation. He was even able to grin. At-tu's trap would soon be sprung. And unless At-tu was a liar, they were as good as free. For a single look had told Pratt that the side he was on was more vulnerable to escape than the opposite end.

THE WALL itself was less smooth, for one thing and for another, shrubs and small rocks projected from the sides, to permit hand and foot-holds. He called the rest to join him. He wondered, however, at the shouts of the watching mob. There was a note of laughter in their voices. The business at hand was more important, at the moment, than the shouts of those above.

Pratt took the lead nor was there any question in the minds of the others that it was not right that he should do so. A thick-branched shrub hung a few feet over his head. Warily, he looked at it for a moment, as if he thought it was some kind of trap placed there deliberately to entice him. Then taking his courage in hand, he leaped lightly for it. It bent for the barest instant beneath his weight, then held!

From then on it was a simple matter of climbing, using the rocks and shrubs as rungs in a ladder. Within the space of several minutes they had all reached the level ground above the pit. A great cheer rang out as the last of the prisoners reached safety. A derisive cheer.

They looked about them curiously. From the opposite end of the pit, it looked as though the cliffs were a long way from the edge. Now they saw that there was a distance of perhaps fifteen feet from the edge to where the cliffs began their smooth and steep-sided climb. They were no longer worried about the cliffs. All they had to do was walk around the rim and to the other end and they were free.

Shouts rang out!

"Over here!"

"This way!"

"Come ahead. You've made it!"

And once again. Pratt detected that note of derision in their voices. Instantly, he made up his mind. Something was wrong!

"Wait men! Let's look around, first."

But only Jama-at, Laeri and Moglu heeded his advice. The rest ran around the rim, some on one side, the others around the opposite end. All met the same fate! They hadn't progressed more than ten feet in either direction, when the ground literally ate them up. This time there was no gradual disappearance. They disappeared instantly. Little puffs of smoke marked where their bodies had sunk from view.

It was then that the four who remained noticed the bones. Skeleton shapes strewed the ground to either side of where they stood. Nor did they have to search far for the reason. These bones were all that was left of those who had elected to stay. A bitter smile played around Pratt's mouth. So that was why the crowd had shouted so derisively. There was a way of escaping the pot. But only to land in the fire. Only this time the fire was above the pot.

The four looked at each other in consternation. For a second, indecision swayed Pratt. He *knew he* could escape! It was only the human impulse, that the fit shall survive, which had given him pause. He knew that with the fifteen feet of running space that he had, it would be a simple matter to leap the pit. And knew, also, that At-tu would keep his word. Yet, these men were now his friends. He had to devise some means of effecting their escape also.

THE THREE moonmen squatted on their heels. Pratt thrust his hands into his pockets. He felt the package of cigarettes and pulling it out, lit up. Exclamations of wonder fell from their lips at his strange act. But Pratt had become transformed. Gone was the bitter look, the drawn expression. Moglu was on his way to the rescue!

"Master!" the voice had projected itself into his mind. "I am at the far edge of the city."

Pratt started to give him an order, then remembered what had happened to the animal and its rider.

"Moglu! Listen carefully! Do not enter that way! Drive around to the hills behind the city." He looked above him to see if he could find some sort of landmark to which he could direct Moglu. The cliffs seemed denuded to vegetation. Then he espied it. The cliff just to their right had a peculiarly shaped boulder at its top. "We're at the bottom of the cliff to the left of the one with the strange-shaped boulder at its top."

"I hear you, Master," came Moglu's acknowledgement.

The time passed in interminable measure. They watched Pratt pace about in curious wonder. To the rest, it was only a matter of time until they either starved to death or chose to commit suicide. They couldn't understand the tenseness Pratt was showing. They knew their case was hopeless. Suddenly Pratt lifted his head in an attitude of intent watchfulness.

Cocking his head to one side, he listened again for that sound which had dimly come to his ears. Then his eyes crinkled at the corners. Moglu had come through! There had been the unmistakable sound of the truck motor from somewhere above. Then Moglu's voice came to them:

"Master. I am here."

Their joy was short-lived at his appearance, however. For they weren't the only ones who were conscious of the strange vehicle and its driver. At-tu and his minions had also seen him. Simultaneously with his voice, a shower of spears fell among them. At-tu was not going to let them escape that way.

Quickly, Pratt gave directions:

"The hose alongside the truck body! Attach it to the winch."

Moglu's voice was a plaintive sound:

"What do you mean?"

There was no time for detailed explanations. Already the spears were falling too close for comfort. They were kept busy hopping about in their desperate efforts to escape the long metal-tipped shafts.

"Never mind," Pratt shouted. "Just drop the hose over the cliff and hold on to the other end."

The four-inch wide hose snaked down the side of the cliff—just fifteen feet short of their reach.

Pratt came to an instant decision.

Standing directly below the hose, he said:

"Laeri. You first."

Maeri's brother looked at him in wonder. What did he mean, 'you first?'

Pratt didn't wait for Laeri to figure out his meaning. Reaching forward, he jerked Laeri to him and bending, placed his hands together to form a sort of stirrup. Laeri caught his intention instantly. Lifting his leg, he put his foot onto the waiting palms. With a single, tremendous heave, Pratt threw Laeri upward. Jama-at gasped at the display of strength. For Laeri's body had gone even higher than the hose's end.

LAERI grasped the thick rubber hose and began the ascent to the cliff top where Moglu strained against the weight of the climbing man.

Jama-at was next. He too found sanctuary on the cliff top. But Pratt was faced with a problem in Moglu. When he tried to heave the immense body of the giant, it proved to be an impossibility. And to make matters worse, the aim of At-tu's men was improving. Twice, spears had fallen too close for comfort.

Once again, Pratt was faced with a hard decision. And this time the odds were altogether against him. Throwing a, "wait here," to Moglu, Pratt leaped for the hose and scrambled up its length. Arriving on top, he turned to the giant holding the hose and said:

"Lower yourself over the side. I'll hold onto your legs. That way he'll be able to reach the hose."

Bracing himself against a rock outcropping, Pratt held tight to the oak like legs of Moglu. In a few seconds he felt an immense weight take hold of the hose. Slowly, exercising all the care and strength at his command, Pratt drew back. His arms felt as though they were being pulled from their sockets at the tremendous load they had to bear. Once, his right leg slipped in a smooth spot in the soil. Throwing himself on one knee, he recovered his balance. Then, with a patience he never knew he possessed, Pratt came erect once more and continued the hazardous task he had undertaken.

Back, inch by inch he went, until the first of the giants appeared on the cliff top. Then it was easier. For then there were two men pulling at the hose.

Pratt breathed in long, gasping breaths. They gathered around him and gave voice to their admiration. He made light of his feat. Already his mind had a new problem. One they'd completely forgotten in the excitement of the escape. Maeri! She was still prisoner.

At-tu still held the trump card.

"I would put the whole city to the sword and flame," Jama-at savagely snarled.

Laeri was silent but his glowering features spoke louder than words of how he felt. Pratt could only feel the bitterness of their position. The cigarette, which had remained between his lips through all that had taken place, had gone out. He removed it and started to throw it from him—and stopped as abruptly as if he had been struck by lightning. Almost immediately, however, he rejected what had come into his mind.

Jama-at, shrewdly guessing that whatever had made Pratt pause as he did, must have been of unusual importance, asked:

"What were you thinking of, my friend?"

"I thought I had a way of freeing her," Pratt said.

"Go on," Laeri broke in.

"It's no use. We can't take the chance."

"Why?" they both asked.

"Well, I thought, when Jama-at mentioned flame, that I could provide that. But it might only result in her death."

"Just what had you planned on doing?" Jama-at asked.

"In that truck," Pratt explained, "is enough flammable material to set the whole village ablaze."

"I see," Jama-at said. "And you thought that in the resultant confusion we would engineer her escape. But there is nothing wrong with that."

"Oh yes there is. Two very important things. Why did you think I told Moglu to drive up to the cliffs when the obvious route would have been the way we were brought in? It struck me as queer, then, that At-tu's men gave their animals a free rein. There is only one explanation. That there is no known path to the village. Only those two-legged beasts know the way. And that by instinct only. It would have been suicide for Moglu to have attempted to drive down that path. Reason number two, the truck holds a liquid, which will spread unchecked when ignited. The second reason can be discounted if we could devise some means of getting around the first."

"I think I have the answer to that," said the Moglu who had been driving the truck.

CHAPTER EIGHT

HE HAD extricated himself from the depths of the cab and had joined them, on the lip of the cliff.

They looked up at him expectantly.

"It is obvious, at least to me, that At-tu built his city where he did because it can easily be defended. With only a single means of ingress the attackers would naturally use the obvious road. And knowing the habits of those two-legged beasts, the emri, I know that they travel in single file when arriving at a water hole or when they have reached their corral.

"Therefore the attackers would be engulfed in the quagmire. Let us carry it one step farther. Let us assume that what has attacked the city is a natural enemy. It knows no barrier. For example, a flood. The city lying in a hollow, would be inundated. At-tu is not stupid. He must have devised some means of escape, other than that single path. That means will be shown to us when they are faced with calamity."

Pratt looked at the giant in sheer amazement. The answer he had given to their problem was so simple, yet so brilliant that an immense respect filled Pratt's soul at the giant's reasoning capacity. There was still the chance...but Pratt dismissed it. Maeri was a prize that At-tu would not easily give up.

As one, they ran for the truck. Pratt started to get into the driver's seat but Moglu shoved him gently aside. The 'hole' the giant had made in the cab top, gave Pratt a start. The windshield hung precariously by a couple of brackets. Only a small section of the top remained. There was a sort of lopsided grin on the apelike face of Moglu as he got in through the top, grunting and groaning with the effort.

Laeri, Jama-at and the other giant scrambled onto the trailer and waited with unabashed curiosity for the thing to start. Pratt sat beside the huge figure in the driver's seat. Moglu set the truck into gear and Pratt felt his chin drop. His respect for the giant deepened with every passing mement. He had told Moglu everything about the truck, except the most important thing, the gearshift. Yet the giant had correctly reasoned out the proper procedure of shifting. The truck moved surely and swiftly across the open plain.

The wheel was pressed close against Moglu's belly. But he handled the wheel with a sureness that was astounding. His bare, immense foot pressed the accelerator clear to the floor board. The truck roared out into the night at terrific speed. Moglu drove with an ease that held Pratt spellbound. In less time than he thought it possible, they arrived at the top of the gentle slope leading to the village of tents.

The Earth was setting. They saw by the departing light that there was an unwanted activity in the city. It was apparent that their escape was not to go unpunished. At-tu was preparing to send a party after them.

It took only a few seconds for Pratt to give the necessary instructions. Then while Moglu drove the truck slowly along the slope, the rest ran alongside with the hose playing out as they ran. Pratt sat astride the trailer watching the flow of gas. The sharp, acrid odor of gasoline filled their nostrils. The highly flammable stuff was slowly filling the long depression.

The gauge showed that a thousand gallons had been let loose. Then Pratt shut off the flow.

MOGLU stopped the truck and they gathered around the cab waiting for the next move. Pratt lit a cigarette amid exclamations of wonder. And flipped it far toward the center of the gasoline filled slope. Even before it struck, there was a burst of flame, which rose high above and illuminated the entire vicinity with a scarlet glow.

"Back on the truck," Pratt commanded tersely.

They watched with tensed nerves to see the reaction of At-tu to this danger. Had Moglu reasoned right? Was there an escape outlet?

The moonmen had done their work well. They had spread the gasoline evenly across the depression. A solid sheet of flame stood between them and those below. Pratt felt a quiver of fear when he saw how well they had done. He could not see how anyone could get past it. Already the flame was attacking the first row of tents. They burst into instant flame. And the fire spread with amazing celerity through the village as the liquid sought its own level.

Then, through the smoke, there rode a dozen men. At their head, holding the body of Maeri, was At-tu. A second after their appearance, another body of mounted men came into view. These also rode pell-mell after their leader. The five above were quick to note that they had started from a point just beyond the flame stricken area.

Even as he gave directions to follow, Pratt's keen eyes saw that some of those who had followed At-tu were carrying something behind them.

The truck sped in pursuit. The emri's speed was almost unbelievable. The flaming slope was left far behind and they were almost to where the cliff-like hills began their abrupt ascent when At-tu and his men pulled up. Then it was that those above saw what the last of the mounted men had dragged behind them. It was a sort of carpet.

Two of them, at a distance of perhaps twenty feet apart rode up the slope, dragging the rush-like carpet behind them. When they arrived at the top, they took stakes from their robes and made the carpet fast to the ground. Then at a signal from one of them, the rest rode up on protecting material.

Moglu had parked the truck at a distance from At-tu and his men. For the first time that night, luck favored them. Great clouds obscured the Earth, making it difficult for those below to see Pratt and his friends. The truck had made little noise as it had sped in pursuit. Moglu idled the motor, waiting for further instructions from Pratt.

He was just waiting to see who would be the first to ride up. His eyes lit up when he saw it was to be At-tu and the girl.

"Let's go!" he shouted, slipping out onto the running board.

Moglu divined Pratt's intention. Straight for At-tu the truck roared, throttle wide open this time, the motor roaring in full-throated challenge. Just as they arrived, the clouds parted. At-tu's face showed amazement but no fear. His reaction was instantaneous. His arm fell across the emri's back in a vicious swipe and the startled animal leaped ahead in a single immense bound that put them in advance of the truck.

But their advantage was only momentary. The truck was far faster than the two-legged beast. In a few seconds they were racing alongside. Pratt's lips were parted in a wide grin. He could see the girl, her eyes wide in fear, was held tightly in the crook of At-tu's arm.

Then they were racing even.

PRATT crouched on the running board trying to gauge the exact time when to make his leap. Gently, Moglu maneuvered the truck alongside. And Pratt left his feet in a diving leap just as At-tu drew his sword and swept it over his head and down in a huge swipe. It was too late for Pratt to do anything about it. But just as the arm came down, Maeri struck the descending arm with a quick blow. The sword passed harmlessly over Pratt's head.

The force of Pratt landing against At-tu knocked all three to the ground. The sword knocked from At-tu's hand. When they arose, it was an even match, insofar as weapons were concerned. But only for a minute. Pratt's first savage lunge brought him face to face with At-tu. The Ekfoo chieftain was taller than the Earthman. But there his advantage ended.

Pratt feinted with his left and as At-tu followed the misleading blow and stepped away, Pratt stepped in and to the right. The right cross Pratt drove to At-tu's jaw sent the taller man spinning to the ground. Pratt started toward him once more but stopped at the sound of approaching hoof beats. Simultaneously, there came the warning from one of the men on the truck:

"Quick! The Ekfoos!"

Pratt took hold of the girl's arm and started at a trot for the truck, which had moved off several yards. At-tu lay athwart their path. Pratt was intent on getting the girl on board and was not paying any attention to the inert figure of the Ekfoo chieftain. The first he knew that At-tu was neither unconscious nor dead was when a strong hand grasped his ankle and rolling on it threw him to the ground.

"The truck!" Pratt grunted as he renewed his struggle.

At-tu's fingers wrapped about Pratt's throat. Slowly Pratt's opponent arose still holding Pratt helpless in his grip. Above the strangled beat of his heart and the gasping, tortured sound of At-tu's breathing, Pratt heard the pounding of the emri's hoofs. Held high in the air, his feet dangling above ground, almost powerless to move and knowing that if he did not release the terrible pressure about his throat, he would be dead in short order, Pratt raised both hands high above his head. And brought them down on the skull of At-tu.

At-tu let out a strangled gasp. Then as Pratt struck once more, the Ekfoo's fingers released their death grip for the barest instant. In that second, Pratt drew back his fist and lashed At-tu across the bridge of the nose. At-tu let out an anguished groan and let Pratt fall to the ground. Pratt struck with lightning like suddenness. Two blows, deep into the man's middle sent him staggering. Before he could recover, Pratt hit him again, this time with all the terrific force at his command. The blow took At-tu on the point of the chin. And broke his neck!

Pratt turned then, to find that he had delayed too long. Three of the mounted Ekfoos, swords gleaming, eyes and hearts thirsting for his blood, were on him. Even his speed, blinding though it was could not save him.

THE THREE men rode abreast. They were only a yard from him when, as if it had come from the sky, the gas truck struck into the center of the three. There was the squealing of brakes and Moglu put the truck into reverse, leaving behind the shattered bodies of men and beasts.

Pratt breathed long and slow, savoring each breath as though it were his last. To their left, the sun's huge disk was coming up over the horizon. And behind them was the dim glow of the burning village of the Ekfoos. Maeri snuggled against Pratt, her head on his shoulder. She seemed content there.

For the first time since his arrival on the moon, Pratt felt at peace. It was a strange sort of feeling. He didn't try to rationalize it. He knew only that he was content. Mainly because of the girl whose head was resting against his shoulder.

The others were holding a low voiced conversation. For a while their voices were something foreign, which kept intruding into the mood he was in. Then he became aware of what was being said.

"There is only one thing to do now," Jama-at was saying. "We must get back to Stamat."

"Why?" asked the Moglu driving the truck.

"Because we must let Komu know what we learned."

"About what?"

"The Hammars! They are plotting to conquer Luona. At-tu was the first ruler they approached in their scheme."

Jama-at's words broke the spell Pratt was in. He heaved a sigh so deep it awoke Maeri from the sleep she had fallen into. Pratt's voice held an edge of bitterness as he asked:

"Listen! Don't any of you people here eat? Or is that a lost art on Luona?"

"You are hungry?" Jama-at queried, surprise in his voice.

"Well—I have been hungrier. But if it's a rule that a person has to let three days go by before eating, I guess I'll have to abide by majority."

"It won't be long," Laeri broke in. "We have only thirty mons to traverse before we reach Stamat. There, you will find food in abundance."

Pratt sighed again, this time in contemplative pleasure in the thought of the steak he was going to order.

"Forgive me my question, but where are you from?" Laeri asked, after a few moments.

Pratt grinned humorlessly at the query. It was going to be a job explaining where he was from, how he got to the moon and what he intended doing now that he was here. Laeri's question brought back thoughts of the planet he had left, the people, places and events which he had been part of, while he lived there.

"Me?" Pratt laughed softly. "Guess I might as well tell all. If for no other reason than to get back to the proper perspective. And keep things in balance.

"That body of earth and water which has just set is my home. Pardon me, was my home. Sometime, when the atmosphere is right and we are in the proper conjunction, I will point out the specific point from where I came.

"How or what it was that contributed to my being here, is a mystery. One moment. I was driving a gas truck from Phoenix to Roswell, the next I was here." Pratt shook his head in vexation. It came to him that he had also told Moglu approximately the same story. Was he going to have to repeat it to everyone on the moon?

"So." Laeri said speculation in his voice. "Parta is inhabited. I had always wondered about that." His voice was suddenly eager, boyishly thrilled. "Tell us a little of your life there."

"Yes," said a soft voice from beside his shoulder. "Tell us about yourself."

CHAPTER NINE

UNDER THEIR urging Pratt gave them a pocket version of his life's history.

"There isn't a great deal to tell," he began. "Born in the city of Chicago, twenty eight years ago, I lived most of my life there. Went through the University, played football: it's a sport: and won a Rhodes scholarship to Oxford. Did a paper on the 'Pattern Thinking Processes Of The Ubangis' and got a Ph.D. for it.

"Went out into the world, a full-blown intellectual. And discovered that a Ph.D. didn't pay the grocer's bill. Knocked around for a spell, trying to give my life a more constructive appearance. Discovered that living entailed more than having a knowledge of the literate things. Then I got the job of driving the gas wagon for Mutual Gas. And that my friends, is all there is to my life, past tense.

"Now," Pratt continued. "We come to my life, present tense. I find myself on, as you call it, Luona, but which we term, the moon. Contrary to popular belief, it is inhabited. Further, the physical features of Luona are not as I had been led to believe. And that is a fact to which I can not reconcile myself. For I have seen through a telescope so powerful it was able to show great mountains on the moon's surface, that the greater part of the moon's area was mountainous. Yet all the evidence before my eyes is to the contrary."

"The most logical explanation of that," said the Moglu seated on the trailer, "is that not only were the factors of space involved in your adventure but also of time. Hazarding a guess, I would say that you arrived on Luona several million years in the future. That is in relation to time as it was on Parta."

Pratt thought it over. Moglu had the proper evaluation, he was sure. And was amazed again, that least human looking of all he had come in contact with on Luona, had the most reasoning of minds. He thought also, of the first men he had met, those queer creatures whose means of locomotion was to curl up into a ball and roll along the ground. He wondered who they were and what was their status on Luona?

The thin, ape-like lips of the Moglu driving parted in a grin. He had read Pratt's mind.

"They are the outcasts of this world," he said. "Cannibals by nature, they are a pariah race. Luckily, they are too few to do any harm. No. But we have a people here who are a menace. The Hammars!"

Again the 'Hammars.' Pratt was intrigued. Who were these Hammars that they inspired such fear?

"The Master Race of Luona, they call themselves. Jama-at thinks they came to At-tu with the purpose of involving him in their scheme. But we know differently."

"Huh?"

Moglu was patient.

"Don't you remember? At-tu accused you of being their emissary!"

IT CAME back to Pratt, then. Moglu was right. Then what did Jama-at mean. As if in answer, Jama-at said :

"It was Toat, that spittle-licking, scum, who told us of the Hammars. I thought that At-tu was party to their scheme. It was only natural."

"No one is accusing you of anything," Laeri said gently. "Your loyalty to my father is too well known for anyone to cast doubts on it."

"Let's get back to the Hammars!" Pratt said impatiently. "Why, or rather, how are they a menace?"

"They are the only people on Luona who have some scientific pretensions. I say pretensions because after seeing how matter of fact you have been about this vehicle, which to us is a wondrous thing, I have no doubts but that there are far more amazing things to be found on your planet. There has not been a war on Luona, within the memory of man. We have, however, numbers of warlike people. The Ekfoos, for example. But the reason for war, material gain, is lacking. For the most part, people here lead a simple, unpretentious life. Our cities are not complex things, depending on commerce for their existence. But the Hammars live on the dark side of our planet. Few of us have ever made the journey to their distant land. I have heard however, that there are many marvelous…"

"Hold it, Moglu!" Pratt broke in. The giant's habit of digressing at great length on unimportant things made it an interminable tale. "Just tell me why these Hammars want to conquer Luona?"

"Why? Because they are philosophers, that's why."

The answer stunned Pratt. Certainly it wasn't the answer he had expected. Now that he had been told, it only made the issue more cloudy. Patiently, Pratt continued his interrogation:

"I don't get the connection. What has their philosophy to do with their making war?"

"Their's is a philosophy of force. Peace is static condition. War, on the other hand, involves movement, releases minds from the torpor of safe, easy living. Peoples involved in the strain of conflict, are more healthy because the conditions of war enforce the necessity for thought. All this is quotation, by the way."

Pratt whistled soundlessly. The Lunatic fringe also existed on the moon. And was as capable of as many mad actions as those who had existed on the Earth. Well, it was their show. He didn't want any part of it.

"I'm afraid that isn't possible," Moglu said.

Pratt groaned. The giant had read his mind once more.

"What isn't possible?" Pratt asked.

"Your washing your hands of the whole matter and saying it's none of your affair. Had you been able to sit in this vehicle for the rest of your life on Luona, then it could be, but since you have participated in events you must continue to do so. Whether or not you want to participate has no bearing on matters."

"Okay," Pratt grunted sourly. "All I've got to say is, that it's a hell of a state of affairs when the slave tells his master what to do." It had come to him that Moglu and Maeri were his slaves, by their own admission.

"It is an old custom but one which no longer has any validity," Moglu gently explained.

SOMEHOW, Pratt felt better at the words. The thought of Maeri as anyone's slave was abhorrent to him. As for

Moglu, Pratt felt the greatest respect for his intelligence. One thing however, which was proving irksome. Moglu's ability to read his mind. Thinking was no longer a private concern. And there were times when a man wanted to be alone with his thoughts.

"Very well, then. I shall stop being a minority of one," Pratt fell in with Moglu's reasonable demand. "Lead on Mac Duff. My steed and I will follow, wherever you lead." He patted the dashboard as though it was the flank of a horse.

The sun was now well above the horizon. Pratt looked curiously about him. The flatness had given way to rolling, hilly country, much like that of southern Illinois. Once he saw a group of strange animals at the edge of the forestland. As the strange vehicle approached, they made off with queer piercing shrieks. Then they came to a wide river. Bluffs lined the opposite end as far as the eye could see. Pratt could see no bridge or other sign of a way of crossing the river. Moglu continued driving so Pratt gathered that there was a way across.

The road, if the belt of sand they were on could be called that, led upward. Pratt, looking ahead, saw only the flat side of one bank and the top of the bluffs bisecting the horizon. Then they were over the rise and rolling down hill. And Pratt saw the bridge.

It was just a plain affair, wooden and rising in a slow arch across the river at a narrow part. Moglu made the turn and they drove across and in between the narrow defile of the bluffs at that point. The hills rose sheer to either side of them for as far as Pratt could see.

"It is not far now," Maeri said. She had been watching Pratt and had surmised that he had been thinking of how long the journey would last.

He turned and grinned at her. She was a funny sort of girl. Quiet, she rarely intruded in his thoughts. It was a nice trait, that. Nicer than most of the other girls he had known. He closed his mind quickly at the thought. He remembered what had happened when he thought of the comparison between her kiss and the others.

He thought it odd they could not always read his mind. Still, they were able to get through frequently enough to make it embarrassing. And something else. How was it they knew English? Or he knew their language? He was sure that Moglu would have the answer.

"Ah!" Maeri exclaimed suddenly.

He returned to the present and saw her eyes were affixed on something close by.

It was a sign, fixed to a post. The sign read:
Stamat: Ten mons.

IT GAVE him a start. A signpost! But why? It was obvious that there were no motor vehicles in the land or Moglu would not have been so amazed at the truck. More, Laeri and Jama-at had also shown the same feelings on seeing it for the first time. Suddenly he burst into uproarious laughter. Moglu looked down at him in surprise. But his curiosity had to wait for an explanation. The bond between them, which made for telepathic communication, was shut off for the moment. Otherwise the giant would have known that Pratt laughed because he thought it funny that such a simple thing as a signpost should have made him imagine devious reasons for it.

The hills spread, as though a giant hand had pushed them apart. The road also widened until it was a broad, smooth thoroughfare. Pratt's eyes went wide as he saw what lay in the near distance, Camelot! If not the abode of the knights of the Round Table, then certainly an excellent imitation.

A large city lay revealed to their eyes. Turreted towers, stone houses, reminding Pratt of an English scene, the whole perched in a valley. Pastoral Beauty, the like of which he did not associate with what he had seen of the rest of Luona. Suddenly Moglu applied the brakes. The giant's eyes were narrowed in speculation.

Pratt followed his gaze and saw approaching, a group of men whose strange attire made him blink. The illusion of Camelot was complete. For clattering toward them were hundreds of mounted knights, complete in armor.

Maeri turned and shouted to her brother:

"Father! Look, Laeri."

"I see," said her brother. Pratt could see the broad grin on his face.

The horsemen came to a clattering stop several yards before they reached the truck. It was evident they were wary of this strange thing. Then the leading horseman saw Laeri, perched on the trailer. Setting spurs to his horse, he came up at a gallop, to come to a sliding, dust-enclouded halt.

The man in armor raised the visor of his helmet and revealed a bearded face, whose stern visage was made redeemable by a pair of gentle gray eyes.

Maeri leaped from the cab and ran toward him. In a second the man was off the six-legged steed and had thrown his arms about the girl. Laeri, Jama-at, and Pratt joined them. Holding the girl at arm's length, her father asked:

"Where did you find her? And what happened to you two? Your armor, where is it?"

"One question at a time, father. But first, let me introduce...what is your name? He turned to Pratt in bewilderment.

"Theodore Pratt Marsh. I imagine we were a little too busy to bother with the formalities of introductions."

Laeri grinned crookedly.

"Yes, I guess we were. Father, this is the man who saved not only the life of your daughter but ours as well."

Laeri's father thrust out a gauntleted hand. Pratt, who had watched the powerful embrace with which Komu had greeted his children had felt misgivings for their safety. Hesitantly, he put his hand forward and was surprised to find it clasped in a strong yet *fleshy* grip. He gave the gauntlet a look of suspicion. It had the appearance of metal. And all around him, he could hear the sounds of clanking armor. Another mystery which would have to wait for a solution.

CHAPTER TEN

SEVERAL of the men had gathered about the truck and were making either complimentary or mystified remarks about it. Komu, his arms around Laeri and Maeri, his arms forward for a closer examination.

"He comes from another world," Laeri said blandly.

"Yes. Isn't it wonderful, father?" Maeri chimed in.

"So? Another world, eh? Hmm. Well, Theodore Pratt Marsh, I can only say that you have my heart-felt gratitude for your great deed and that whatever your wish shall be my command."

There was no sense in trying to pass off what he had done as being of no consequence. These two, Laeri and the girl were the children of a reigning chief. Pratt murmured something something about them being 'too kind,' then lapsed into silence.

"But tell us, mighty Komu," Jama-at asked curiously, "have you brought out the entire army to seek us? Or is there another reason for their being with you."

A stern look came into the kindly eyes of the man in armor. His lips sheared a straight line across the lower part of his face.

"Aye," he said. "There was another reason. Shortly after Laeri and you left to seek Maeri, an emissary of my friend,

Horta came to me with dire tidings. The Hammars were putting into reality the threats they had been making through the years. A vast horde of them have debauched from the dark side of their lands and are marching on the rest of our world. As time went by. I became fearful that they had taken Maeri hostage. And so you found me on the road to meet them and take vengeance."

"Alone?" Laeri asked incredulously.

"How do you mean? I have my entire army with me."

"Surely we need more than that," Jama-at said softly.

"So Horta said," Komu replied. "But he wanted time to gather allies. I told the emissary that I would seek the Hammars out and give them battle, thus delaying them until we could muster enough to face them."

"It *is* good strategy. But will it serve the purpose for which it was intended? Have you received reports on how large an army they have? Did the emissary tell how Horta came by his information? Did he..."

"Enough! Do you take me for an idiot? Yet—you are right. Perhaps I was too hasty. Coming as it did, on the heels of Maeri's strange disappearance, I surmised—well, it's no matter now. You are all safe."

"For the moment," Jama-at said in reminder. "May I suggest that the army return to Stamat? If the Hammars are on the march, we will do better than go to meet them in this manner."

Pratt waited, one foot on the running board, for them to make their minds up. He stepped within the cab when he saw Komu nod in agreement to Jama-at's suggestion. Maeri, her brother and Jama-at took their places once again and the cavalcade turned back to Stamat.

PRATT waited until the sub-chiefs had said their say. He looked about the huge round table, around which were gathered all the important people of Stamat. At the head sat Komu. Pratt had listened with mixed feelings to the talk that had gone the round of the table. A great deal of it had been childish. Of them all, only Komu and Jama-at had any idea of a plan to put into use against the invaders.

"May I say something?" he asked, not being able to hold his feelings in abeyance longer.

Komu nodded gravely for him to have his way.

"It is evident that war is something about which you people know nothing."

Some of the men gathered there made as if to stop Pratt.

"Let him have his say!" Komu thundered.

Silence fell.

"It is true," Pratt went on, unperturbed at the interruption, "that I know very little of these Hammars. But, from what I have gathered listening to you here, I know enough. That they come from the dark side of Luona: that they have the reputation of being wizards: that they are not many in numbers: and that the rest of the peoples of Luona are afraid of them. Hell! I'd say they had you buffaloed!"

Expressions of wonder showed on many faces at Pratt's incomprehensible phrase. He went on without pause:

"Since, by your own evidence, they come from a long way off, I gather that it will take them a long time to reach their nearest goal. Their only means of transportation are these six-legged animals you call, *minas*. As for their weapons, the sword and bow is as far advanced as you people have gone in the art of war. So that in the final showdown, it will be a matter of man against man. Therefore, I have a suggestion to make.

"While you plan and gather a sufficiency of allies, I will go out to meet them, see how large a force they have, reconnoiter the ground, get the lay of the land, as it were."

Silence greeted his words. But in the faces of Komu, Jama-at and several others was to be seen that which told Pratt that his plan *had* found favor.

"Do you plan on going alone?" Komu asked, musingly.

"No. I thought of taking the Moglu. They know the land and one of them can spell me in driving."

"Father!" Laeri said unexpectedly. "I would also go."

His father nodded.

"Very well. You will be properly outfitted with all the gear that you may need. When do you plan on leaving?"

"As soon as I can."

"Very well. Laeri...see to it that all is taken care that you may leave tonight."

Laeri leaped from his seat, a broad grin on his face. Running around the table until he reached Pratt, he took hold of his arm saying joyously:

"Wonderful! Follow me, my friend."

Pratt shook Komu's hand in farewell. As he passed Jama-at the warrior stopped him and said:

"Careful! They are treacherous, the Hammars. And before you reach them, you will have to traverse a dangerous land."

Pratt's eyebrows reached skyward at Jama-at's words. Laeri, dragging at his arm, prevented him from asking what the other meant. He filed the words for future reference, however. The Moglu, who seemed to know everything would have the answer to that.

"Wait!" Pratt commanded as Laeri started in the direction of the armory. "I—I want to say goodbye to Maeri."

Laeri patted his shoulder and said: "I'll wait here for your return."

SHE WAS seated by the window, when he entered her room. A serving maid was brushing the long blond locks of her hair. In the strong sunlight, her hair had a golden tinge. The sound of the door opening made them turn. Maeri smiled gently on seeing him. The maid, seeing the smile, murmured something and slipped shyly from the room.

"Look!" she said, pointing to something that was taking her attention beyond the window.

He stepped to her side and followed her gaze.

Below, in the immense yard of the palace, were gathered a great throng of warriors. Some were mounted on the six-legged *minas*, others were afoot and still others were on animals, the like of which Pratt had never seen. There was a constant eddying movement, a display of colors of every hue of the rainbow. It was the second day since Pratt had first set foot in Stamat. And all that morning and the day before men had been arriving in a steady stream, summoned by Komu and his friend. Many of these people carried pennants, flags and insignia of their cities.

He turned his glance from the outside and centered it on the entranced girl.

"Maeri," he said softly.

She turned swiftly to him.

"Yes?"

"I am going away."

Her eyes went wide.

"What do you mean?"

He bit his lips. It was going to be difficult to tell her, he realized. If for no other reason than this was the first that she was going to hear of his feelings.

"It was decided that I and the Moglu were to go out and...

The color fled from her cheeks, leaving them more pale than the rose and twice as lovely. There was no need for him to go on. She knew what he had to say. Silently, she arose and walked straight into his arms. He held her away from him and said:

"Don't worry! Now that I've found you, there isn't anything in this world that'll keep me from coming back."

She wasn't an Earth woman, weak, neurotic. She was of Luona where life was hard and decisions had to be made whose consequences could be death. Gently, she kissed him once again and whispered:

"I will be here…whenever you return."

Turning, he walked from the room. Nor did he turn for a last look.

The smile Laeri greeted him with was wiped from the boy's lips when he saw the stern look on Pratt's face.

"This way," he said in a low voice, leading him toward the armory.

IT WAS and immense room, high vaulted, stone-walled. Great racks held spears in orderly rows. Other racks held an assortment of swords. The warrior in charge sized Pratt up and in a trice had him fitted up in a suit of the strangely light armor. It was as smooth and light as the finest silk.

"How effective is this stuff?" Pratt asked.

"It will turn the sharpest sword point," Laeri answered.

Pratt's lips pursed.

"I suppose you know what you're saying," he said grudgingly. "Still…"

Laeri smiled knowingly.

"Have no fear," the other answered. "It will serve the purpose for which it is intended."

"What of the Moglu?" Pratt asked, thinking of their large bulk.

Laeri shook his head. "We have nothing that will fit them," he said. "I suppose, because the thought that they would never be our allies, never occurred to us."

The armorer, who had gone off in search of a sword for Pratt, returned just then, bearing a large, two-edged blade.

"Heft it," he commanded.

Pratt took hold of the hilt, which was large enough to accommodate both hands, and swung it around his head in a clumsy gesture. But clumsy as it was, the blade hummed in the air. The armorer's eyes went wide on hearing the sound.

"By my father's loins," he whispered in an awe-struck voice. "It will go ill with any man who falls in that blade's path."

Laeri shook his head in amazement.

Pratt was embarrassed by their display of wonder. He attempted to pass it off as nothing. "Look," he said, "after all, you have to take into account the fact that things here don't have the weight for me that they have for you."

But they continued to shake their heads in wonder at his feat. The armorer patted his shoulder, surreptitiously feeling of a bicep as he did so.

Pratt's embarrassment was dissipated by the entrance of the Moglu. The two giants stood silent in respectful attitudes, waiting for their leader's command.

"Well," Pratt said hastily. "Might as well be off, eh Laeri?"

Laeri nodded and made for the exit.

Pratt's heart gave a lift at sight of the gas truck. It was his only link with a past that was forever gone. Now that he knew that matters between him and Maeri were as they were, he no longer cared ever to leave Luona. There were no ties to return to on the Earth.

He smiled at sight of the cab. The Moglu had been busy. Only the windshield remained. And he saw too, that the entire truck had been covered with the silk-like material that passed for armor. It was a clever move, designed to protect the truck from being pierced by an arrow or spear.

The truck had been brought into the enclosure by one of the giants. Pratt seated himself in the cab with one of the giants beside him. Laeri and the other sat on an improvised seat just behind the cab. Slowly, Pratt maneuvered the truck around until it was facing the opening in the enclosure. Then he looked up toward the window of Maeri's apartment. Nor was he disappointed. She was leaning from the window and at sight of him she waved her hand. He answered the gesture and gave the truck a burst of gas. It sped from the courtyard to the accompaniment of the cheers of the assembled warriors. Pratt had an idea that it would be some time before he saw them again.

CHAPTER ELEVEN

THE NOW familiar countryside sped by in its rather monotonous sameness. Moglu was driving. Pratt had given the wheel over to the giant right after they had left Stamat.

"Any idea how long it will take?" Pratt asked after they had spanned the bridge leading to Stamat.

"It depends on how swiftly the Hammars have moved," the giant answered.

They rode in silence for a while. Then Pratt decided it was as good a time as any to have the questions that were bothering him answered.

"You speak an excellent English. Where did you learn it?"

The prognathus jaw of the giant spread wide in a grin.

"You speak an excellent Luonian," he answered. "I might ask you the same question." He laughed softly, then went on:

"As a matter of fact, neither of us speak what we think of as language. It's a thought process too quick for human perception. Our thoughts are instantly translated into sound. What you hear are those sounds. To you they are as you call them, English. To us they are Luonian. But here, they are universally understood."

Insofar as Moglu was concerned, it was a simple explanation of a simple fact but to the Earthman's more than ordinary grasp of things it was far more complex than Moglu made it out to be. Jama-at's warning came to mind, then.

"What sort of country do we go through?" he asked.

"How do you mean?"

"Jama-at mentioned something of the danger we would encounter," Pratt said. "I wondered what he meant by that."

Moglu's face sobered. He remained silent for several moments collecting his thoughts and putting them in order. He knew it was going to be difficult to explain what Jama-at meant. The sign that fell from his lips held an odd note. An exasperated note.

"To begin," Moglu offered in explanation, "I must clear up one or two things for you. For one thing, there has never been any close contact between nations. Each has been self-sufficient. To such a degree, indeed, that any intrusion, even of accident, has been regarded with suspicion. In the end, it has led to a sort of aggregation of nations and peoples. Some of the nations on Luona have never permitted their peoples to go beyond the borders of their own lands. So that a great deal of this planet's surface is a mystery to them.

"Now that a war has been declared, all of that is going to prove of detriment to us. For we are moving into regions of hearsay. From now on I can only say that it has been told that so and so is the case. Or that it has been said, these people are like this."

"Well," Pratt interrupted. "What about those, 'rollers' I met? And the Ekfoos? You seemed to know a great deal about them."

"We do," Moglu said. "But that is because they are on the light side of Luona. Very soon we will enter the dark portion. That is the side which is a mystery to us."

A PHENOMENA of nature took place then, which took Pratt', attention from Moglu. The sun had sank beneath the horizon. But the now familiar Earth glow was missing. It was a region of gloom. Shadows blended in such a way that it was difficult to tell the real from the imaginary. Pratt flicked the headlights on.

Deeper and deeper into the land of gloom sped the truck. Here and there, trees raised their ghostly shapes across the headlight's beam. Moglu drove as casually as if it was broad daylight. Pratt realized after a few moments that the gloom was not as intense as he had imagined it to be on first glance. As a matter of fact it proved to be a sort of twilight land. Trees, rocks, and physical things were slightly distorted. But after he had accustomed himself to it, the land proved far less fearsome than it had been at first.

"It was from this part of the world that tidings came of the invasion," Laeri said.

Pratt looked up and asked:

"Oh yes, Laeri. I meant to ask. How did this Horta hear of it?"

"Seems that these border folks are the link between the rest of Luona and us. They heard it from some who live deeper in the land of darkness."

Pratt had not noticed that they were on rising ground. The labored sound of the motor made him turn his attention to Moglu. The giant's face reflected a concentration that was compelling. Suddenly, Moglu slammed on the brakes and shut the motor simultaneously. The twin beams of lights flickered off.

"Listen!" Moglu whispered.

Pratt strained his attention to the task. The air was warm, quite fragrant with the smell of flowers. It was still. The peep of birds could be heard. He could hear nothing else. Then he heard it! Or rather *felt* it. Sound that was as palpable as the wind that brushed his suddenly wet cheek. He realized the wetness was of sweat.

The strange sound was all about them. It was to be heard from beyond the snub nose of the radiator: from behind the sloping back of the trailer. On their left and to their right. It enveloped them like an evil blanket. Pratt felt the hackle rise on his nape.

"What is it?" he whispered hoarsely.

"I don't know," came the equally hoarse response.

The strange sound came closer. Now they could characterize it. It was the sound of wind! But of wind they had never believed possible. Pratt looked up and saw that the sky was obscured by clouds. The darkness complete, intense with blackness that was impenetrable.

Then the wind struck them.

So terrific was the blast that the truck swayed drunkenly in its grip.

"Start the motor!" Pratt screamed.

But his words were torn from his lips and never reached the giant. Pratt reached down and turned the key. Moglu understood the gesture and pushed at the starter button. The meter caught with a roar. Moglu put it into gear and they were off.

He had stalled the truck on the top of a small hill where the wind was able to lash them without mercy, and did. Dust, pebbles, earth struck them with the force of hailstones. They could only cower as low as possible against the wind.

PRATT and Laeri had the protection of their armor. The visors of their helmets gave them protection. But the Moglu had nothing. Further, their added height made it impossible for them to escape the hurricane blasts. Already the giant was finding it impossible to drive any farther. Pratt knew that the truck had to keep moving. Yet if he attempted to leave the wind would carry him away as if he were no more than a leaf torn from a branch. Instead, he lifted with a display of strength that amazed even him, who had become somewhat accustomed to it, Moglu from his seat and holding the giant body aloft, slid into the seat occupied by the other. Moglu fell with a crash into the vacated seat.

No sooner did Pratt solve that difficulty than another presented itself. The wind was becoming stronger with the passing minutes. The truck labored against the almost supernatural strength of the blasts, making so little progress that it was difficult to tell whether they were moving or not. More, at times the wind was so strong that it tipped the truck.

Pratt knew that because of the gas it would not require much to tip it over. Yet no matter what direction they faced the wind met them head on. Once more the truck tipped. Frantically, Pratt twisted the wheel in the direction in which the wind had swung the body. An interminable age went by before he felt the truck right itself. He turned in the interval between that blast and the next, to find that the giant was no longer beside him. He felt, rather than saw another come into the vacated seat. It was Laeri!

"Stop it!" Laeri shouted.

"What?" Pratt screamed in answer.

"This—this vehicle! The Moglu has seen something ahead. He and the other have gone to investigate."

Pratt took it out of gear but left the motor on. The two peered beneath the visor of their helmets, trying to see where the giants had gone. It was almost impossible, what with the dust and dirt flying about. Then Pratt saw a shape at his side of the cab.

"Move over!" A voice said.

It was one of the Moglu.

Pratt did as he was ordered. The giant took command. He steered the truck to the right. Where he was going was mystery to the other two. But it was evident that he knew. For in a few moments they reached an area of calm.

Pratt and Laeri got out of the truck, slowly, laboriously. They moved stiff-legged as if their strength had been expended in some physical struggle. Pratt threw his visor up with a tired gesture. Looking about he discovered that the explanation of the calm was quite simple. The Moglu had spotted the outlines of a hill and had driven the truck into its lea. And although the wind could still get at them, it had lost most of its effect.

The two giants were seated on the ground. Pratt saw that they were exhausted by their battle against the wind. The two in armor joined them. They sat there for a long time, waiting and wondering when the hurricane would abate.

"Look!" Laeri exclaimed, after a while.

Pratt followed his gaze. Their outstretched legs were being covered with dirt. It had been so gradual a process that none had noticed it. They all recognized the danger, however. There was no way of measuring how fast the dirt was piling up. But in the short while their fascinated glances watched, they saw that the tops of their legs were already covered.

They scrambled erect and looked wonderingly at each other. In each glance was the same question, how long could they remain in safety? Desperately, Pratt regarded the hillside. Perhaps there was safety in it somewhere? He lifted his hand in a gesture of command and they followed as he set out to investigate the possibilities of this thought.

Once again it was one of the giants who found what they hoped to. Because of the armor Pratt and Laeri wore, it was impossible for them to have felt the air escaping from the fissure in the hillside.

ONE BY ONE they entered the narrow gap into the Stygian darkness of they knew not what. Pratt berated himself for not bringing his flashlight. It was too late to go back, however. The silence was almost frightening after the maelstrom of sound from beyond. Gradually they became used to it. And to the gloom of the cavern. They had been gathered in a group, as if in the proximity of their numbers, there was safety and sanity. For somehow, the cave had a frightening effect on them.

It was the Earthman who first recovered his courage.

"We act like a gang of frightened school kids," he remarked caustically. "It's only a cave."

Laeri's voice when he answered trembled slightly, but his words were brave enough.

"Yes. I always wondered why just being in the dark was frightening. Perhaps it's because our mothers used to scare us in our childhood with tales of what hideous things were to be found?"

"Hmmm. Maybe," Pratt answered absent-mindedly. He was staring toward an odd phenomena. Light, pale and phosphorescent, was streaming from the darkness in the cave's depths. "Wonder what that is?" he asked speculatively.

No one seemed to have a reasonable answer.

"Might as well see," he offered in suggestion.

He took the lead when they fell in with his suggestion. The source of the strange luminescence proved to be further afield than they thought. And the cave proved to be deeper than they had imagined on first entering it. At first they walked in single file, close on each other's heels. Then, as the cave widened and the light grew somewhat stronger, they separated into two ranks. The giants exclaimed in wonder as their startled eyes beheld the wonders of the strange cave unfold before them.

"Look!" one of them exclaimed.

"Why—it's a statue!" said Laeri, peering closely at what Moglu had pointed out.

They gathered around the odd figure. As tall as a man, it was a perfectly simulated figure, complete even to garments. But the most astonishing thing about the statue was its eyes. They seemed alive! On closer examination, they proved to be some sort of glass which, reflecting the light, made them look alive. They continued in their search and in a few minutes came upon another of the figures. Then, at regular intervals, they met more of them until, with a suddenness that was startling, they ceased.

"Do you know how many of them there were?" one of the giants asked.

None besides himself had bothered to count.

"Two hundred," he said.

They continued with their investigation, talking over in whispers the mystery of the statues. Soon they fell silent. The weird luminescence increased. It festooned the ceiling, dripped from the walls, left glowing footprints behind them. It increased, yet, somehow never grew brighter.

On and on they went, nor could any of them say how long they had walked. It must have been for a long time because Pratt began to feel the gnawing pain of hunger. Yet he would not turn back.

CHAPTER TWELVE

AS abruptly as they had entered the region of the strange light, they left it. The cleavage was complete! Behind them was the glow, in front was a half-gloom, in which could be seen, but faintly, the contours of the cave.

They stopped, as one, at the boundary. Four heads turned simultaneously to the rear. It was as if they possessed a common consciousness, which had told them that ahead lay danger. And once again, Pratt took the lead. Straight into the murky gloom. Fearfully, the rest followed.

The gloom lightened, became gray, then almost as light as day without sunlight. They perceived in the new light that the cave was narrowing. They saw at a distance, that they were coming to a bend in the cave. Pratt began to wonder, belatedly, when their journey would end. He hoped that it lay beyond the turning. Then they were faced with the bend. It was abrupt: right-angled.

They pressed close to each other, regarding the turn with looks bordering on suspicion. For it was evident that it was a man-made turn. The sheer sides of the wall ahead were of concrete or some similar stone. Taking a deep breath, Pratt moved into the bend.

It proved to be a tunnel a few yards long. At its end was a flight of stone stairs. They led upward. The four gathered at the bottom of the flight and looked questioningly at each other for the space of several seconds. Laeri grinned and shrugging his shoulders said in an amused tone:

"What have we to lose? We've come so far without mishap. No reason to stop, now."

Pratt answered the boyish grin. The Moglu remained silent. But their features were tight in strain. It was obvious that they were suspicious of all the mystery.

Pratt continued to grin as he started up the stairs, but Laeri noticed that he had drawn his sword. He followed suit, as he trod hard on the Earthman's heels. The stairs spiraled upward and they followed its circular bent. They ended on a wide platform. And at the end of the platform was another series of stone stairs!

They regarded the stairs with bewildered looks.

"This is silly!" Pratt said aggrievedly. "We go up. Then we've got to go down. For what reason?"

Laeri shrugged his shoulders. He echoed Pratt's sentiments. But the Moglu found an intent behind the bewildering paradox of the stairs, that was not of innocence.

"Wait!" one of them said, as Pratt started down.

He paused, waiting to hear what the giant wanted.

"It isn't silly," Moglu said gently. The other giant nodded in agreement. "On the contrary, I am beginning to see a purpose behind all this. What that is, I don't know. Perhaps it's instinct. At any rate, let me suggest that instead of all of us going down, let me be the one. And if it's safe, I'll return. If not, you will know by my absence, that something is wrong. Remember, we have a mission. My loss will be a small thing."

Pratt bit his lip. Moglu's action was heroism of an extreme sort. He saw then, for the first time, that although he and Laeri were armed, the giants had no weapons whatever. Pulling his sword free of the scabbard, he handed it to the giant. Silently, Moglu accepted the weapon—and started the descent.

PRATT had accepted the cave and what they had seen there, as a sort of something to pass the time until the windstorm passed. Now, there swept over him the certainty that something deeper than chance was at work. The stairs and the statues were evidence that human hands had been at work. It was natural that the questions of why and who should be asked.

A feeling of the deepest revulsion and fear suddenly swept over him. It was as if he had been brushed with something unclean. He found that his jaw was tightly locked as if he was expecting contact with a force that he feared had yet to fight.

The stairs made a turn shortly after the top. Darkness masked the mystery of what lay below, hid Moglu completely. They waited above, tense, expectant, not knowing for what but hoping for the best. His fist clenched and unclenched convulsively. The wait became intolerable. And only silence answered the question in his mind.

A voice, magnified ten-fold by the sound chamber of the stair shaft, came booming upward:

"Master! Come below!"

The sudden, booming sound gave them a start. But from the excited quality of it they gathered that all was well below, insofar as danger was concerned. They trotted down the stairs hard on each other's heels. And when they reached the level where the giant was, they stopped stock-still and looked open-mouthed at the scene before them.

Pratt was reminded of a theater stage. They were in one wing and stretching before them was the width of the stage. But a stage barren of people. Only the props were there. And what props! Moglu more excited than at any time since Pratt remembered, was motioning them forward. He was standing before a number of the same stone figures they had seen earlier.

It was a vast cavern, man made, hollowed out at what vast effort and to what advantage Pratt could not guess. And the entire cavern was filled with row on orderly row of the stone figures, all male. At a rough guess, he judged there were a thousand of them.

All alike, they looked as if they had been manufactured by some machine. The figures showed a remarkably life-like human delineation. Even the folds of the robes they wore seemed real in the drape of the stone cloth.

Laeri who had interested himself in something else, called excitedly from a far wall:

"Pratt, look!"

They gathered around the excited Laeri. He was pointing to a fixture on the wall. Pratt now saw that there many of the same fixtures fixed throughout the cavern.

"Lumino lights," Laeri said.

"So?"

"This place is inhabited."

"Was," Pratt amended. He pointed to the footprints they had made in the dust. "It's been a long time since anyone was here. The dust in those prints are at least six inches deep. And that makes me wonder. Notice that the walls are of concrete: roof also. So how did dust get into here? There must be an exit."

AS though the words were an order, they set about looking for it. But if there was one it was well concealed. Pratt, tired from the strain, leaned against a section of the wall. It pivoted outward with his weight. He stumbled and slipped to his knees, on the outside. Scrambling erect, he looked dazedly at the blank face of the wall. Then he put his hands against it and pushed. The wall swung on its pivot, revealing the startled faces of his friends.

They came out slowly, looking all the time at the great stone gate. Curiously, they examined it. A foot thick, it had been constructed so cleverly that when it was closed there wasn't a hair-breadth's space between the fittings.

"Now why," asked one of the Moglu, "do I think there is a connection between the wall and the stone figures within?"

Laeri shrugged his shoulders and said:

"Must there be?"

Pratt held his silence but he too thought as the giant did. He realized that a discussion would be speculative and idle. Further, the storm or whatever it was, had passed. The hunger he had begun to know returned. Darkness still covered the land. From what they said, the darkness was eternal. But he saw that it was tempered by a light grayness, which passed for the daylight of this world.

His hunger was the only gauge by which time could be told, as far as he was concerned. Some time during the previous day he had eaten. But since the moon revolved so much slower, more than twenty-four hours had passed.

"My Master hungers," one of the giants said. It was a simple stating of a fact. "Rest here," he went on. "My brother and I will seek food."

They were a pair of grotesque, apelike shapes, moving out into and becoming part of the gray scheme.

The two who remained found a flat boulder on which they seated themselves to await the return of the Moglu.

"These statues puzzle me," Pratt said, returning to the thought uppermost in his mind.

"There are many strange things in this dark world," Laeri observed. "No doubt there is an explanation. Why worry about them? They can do us no harm."

"About these *strange* things, you speak of. How come they are strange? Certainly we haven't gone so far that the nearest people to the dividing line can't have a knowledge of what goes on."

"Perhaps they aren't as curious as you."

"Granted! Yet they have contacts with the Hammars. For it was they who gave warning. Therefore—wait a minute." His brows knit in concentration. Then he slapped his thighs with a gauntleted hand. They rustled with the sound of silk. "Laeri! Who are these people?"

"What people?"

"The ones who have told you of the Hammars."

"They are called, Jannsi."

"And they are the only ones who have seen the Hammars?"

LAERI turned a puzzled glance in Pratt's direction. He couldn't understand what he was driving at.

"So I've been told," he said.

"And I'll wager that whoever else heard of the Hammars, heard of them through the Jannsi. Laeri, the plot is beginning to unfold—but I can't as yet see what's behind it."

"Just what are you driving at? Why it's almost universal knowledge that the—I see." Laeri had suddenly stopped in his reply. Slowly, he went on, "Assuming that...I...hang it, Pratt what could be their reason then, for declaring war? Why there aren't more than a few thousand of them alto- gether."

"I'm beginning to understand, a little," Pratt said, "Look...they spread a rumor of an invasion. As I remember, your father said the invasion was coming from this direction. Therefore they gave him this direction in which to look and move to meet the mythical Hammars. And I'm willing to bet that it was they who originally suggested that he gather all the allies together and move from Stamat."

"Go on," said Laeri.

"Then," Pratt continued, "they would move in. Of course I have no idea why."

"Nor I," Laeri confessed. "But I think the Moglu might have."

"The Moglu? What makes you say that?"

"Their lands adjoin the Jannsi's."

Pratt sighed in exasperation. He felt as if he were one of the pieces of a jigsaw puzzle. And whoever was fitting the pieces together was deliberately putting him first in one position, then another only to confuse him.

There was a crackling sound in the underbrush beyond the boulder on which they were sitting. The giants appeared, carrying the carcass of a small animal between them. They threw the carcass at the feet of the two on the boulder, and kneeling at its side began to dismember and skin the animal. Pratt saw that it resembled an Earth deer.

"How did they do it?" he asked. "Whistle to it?"

"The Akra is one of our most tame animals," Laeri explained. "It will feed from your hand."

"Yes," one of the giants said, grinning. "We fed him— and now it will feed us."

It tasted like venison. The warmth of the small fire the giants had built was welcome against the chill of the bleak wind. Their hunger satisfied, the four relaxed in the warmth.

Once again Pratt brought up the subject of the Hammars:

"Laeri tells me you people have had dealings with the Jannsi," he said.

The ridged and muscled facial flesh wrinkled into new lines as the giant to whom Pratt addressed the remark, turned in his direction.

"It is common knowledge. What makes you ask?"

Pratt then gave him a resume of the conversation he had with Laeri. The two giants nodded somberly at the conclusion.

"Now that you put it in that light," one of them said, "we can see that there has always been something strange in that they seem to be the only ones to have been able to communicate with the Hammars."

"But they seem to be such harmless people," the other giant said. "Why," he broke into hoarse laughter. "Why," he continued, "they are as little children. Not alone in body but in mind as well."

"How's that?"

"It would be rather difficult to explain. You'd have to see them to get an idea of what I mean."

"And a good idea it is," said Pratt. "Suppose we do just that."

"But what about the Hammars?" Laeri asked.

"That is one of the questions our *childish* friends are going to have to answer," Pratt replied.

PRATT turned and walked past them and through the half-open wall.   Laeri sighed resignedly, but followed the Earthman's lead. The Moglu brought up the rear.

Pratt turned and looked back at the narrow fissure in the rock through which the four had just come. Even at the few yards that separated them from it, it was almost invisible. Further, there was a slight overlapping of the surface at that point, making it even more difficult to recognize the fissure for what it was. And with the fact of the constant semi-darkness, it was just sheer chance which had led the Moglu to stumble on it.

The truck was mired almost to the hubs in dust. The Moglu instantly set out to scooping handfuls of it and tossing them aside. Pratt and Laeri used the flat sides of their swords as shovels. It was a labor of necessity. They were a weary four, when the last handful and makeshift swordful had been tossed to the side. Pratt realized he could use a bit of shuteye, then. The giant beside him forestalled any possibility of that by saying:

"Continue in that direction." He pointed ahead. "It will not be long before you will have reached the Jannsi's land—what there is of it."

"Yeah?" Pratt said shortly. Tiredness crept over him with the slow, smoothness of water. Almost, he was indifferent to everything. It all seemed so unimportant beside the greater desire to get some sleep. He wondered when the inhabitants of Luona slept. In the short, or rather long few days of his enforced residence, he had known them to have only a few hours of sleep.

The giant was in one of his chatty moods.

"Eat and sleep. That is the best description of the Jannsi. And think. They sit for hours, and do nothing but contemplate the wonders of creation."

Pratt envied them their ability and time…to find sleep.

The truck rolled on over the smooth sand of the road. Relentlessly, his eyelids closed. The voice of the giant became a lullaby to which Pratt found himself nodding. Once and again his eyes opened wearily. Then they closed in sleep.

He did not know how long he slept. He only knew that he was awake and that the truck had stopped. He surveyed the scene before him through bloodshot eyes. Laeri and the other giant were standing beside the truck.

He joined them. Above them and beyond the shallow bed of what had once been a stream, was a low mesa. They paused above the shallow bank and as they stood there, one of the giants said, casually:

"Best let us make our presence known."

CHAPTER THIRTEEN

THE two started down. Pratt watched them for the barest instant. He smiled shallowly. Those two! They had proved their worth in more ways than one. Even in the small detail of acting as ambassadors…and before Laeri's dumbfounded gaze, Pratt had suddenly and inexplicably leaped after them.

They had gone perhaps twenty feet while the two above had watched. But it wasn't too great a distance for Pratt to jump. In fact, he leaped clear over their heads. Laeri watched them stop short as Pratt's body arched over them and came lightly to rest just past them. He saw the Earthman say something and saw the two shake their heads vigorously. Once again spoke, this time with a vehement shake of his head. He had evidently given an order for the two giants made an about face and the three started back to Laeri.

Perplexed, the son of Komu watched them approach. Why had Pratt made that sudden leap? What had been in his mind? He could tell nothing from their expressions. It was as if they had all assumed the same mask, blank and stolid.

The Moglu stood to one side. Pratt was in profile to Laeri, one side of his mouth down—drawn in half a snarl.

"What's wrong?" Laeri asked.

"We are either fools—or simpletons," Pratt said softly. "That thought came to me as I watched them walk away from us. That thought...and another."

His manner was mystifying in the extreme. And Laeri was the sort of person to whom everything had to be explained.

"Didn't it occur to you," Pratt asked, "that either the Moglu know what they are talking about or they don't? There is no middle way."

Laeri waited for Pratt to continue.

"Don't you see," Pratt said sharply, on seeing the blank look on Laeri's face, "it doesn't add up? They say they are the only ones who can communicate with these Jannsi. Then how did your father's friend hear of the Hammar invasion? How did At-tu? Or Jama-at? None of them mentioned the Moglu. Who volunteered to lead us? The Moglu," he answered his own question. "And now they want to take us to the Jannsi—*but first they must go alone!*"

"You mean they are traitors?" Laeri asked incredulously.

"Worse, maybe."

"What are your intentions?"

Pratt bit his lower lip in vexation. Truth to tell, he didn't know. If he only knew what was behind the Moglu's minds. Perhaps he was wrong about them. But on the other hand, if the circumstances proved them to be traitors...so what? He and Laeri were on the spot anyway. He made up his mind then. Let the giants lead them where they will.

He called them over. They stood silent, glowering, waiting for his decision.

"You have said that you were our friends," he said.

"Yes!" they answered emphatically.

"Very well. Prove it."

They understood his meaning. Turning, they started once again for the Jannsi domain. Pratt and Laeri followed at distance. They had not far to go. Beyond the riverbed lay a broad path, evidence that many people had used it for it was well worn and rutted from the countless steps which had trod it. The path led upward, up the face of the steep but short plateau. The Moglu waited for the other two, when they reached the top.

"We will go together," one of them said.

Pratt nodded in acquiescence.

"It isn't far," said the other giant. "See! There in the center."

IT WAS JUST another shadow to Pratt. Then he saw the outlines more distinctly. The structure he saw puzzled him. Then he knew what it reminded him of. The pueblo, of some of the Arizona tribes. Only in miniature.

He thought it was a matter of perspective. The low-walled series of stone houses were at a distance of about a half-mile. And beyond them he saw the far rim of the mesa, a vague blot on the horizon.

They made for it in single file.

"Ho strangers!" a voice shouted.

And was echoed and re-echoed a thousand times, "Ho strangers!"

The four stopped short at the sudden sound. The Moglu had led them to the lip of a dip in the plateau. It extended downward thirty or forty feet. Below the dip was a cleared area, fully a hundred yards across. The first of the series of pueblos began at the far edge of the clearing. The strange voice had come to them from the bottom of the dip.

"It is the Moglu," one of the giant shouted in reply.

"Who comes with you?" came the query.

"Friends."

"Enter then," came the command.

Pratt kept looking to right and left, as they made their way down the slope. Emptiness met his gaze. The giants continued toward the nearest dwelling, after they reached the bottom, seemingly undisturbed by the voices.

And then with a suddenness that was unnerving, the voices sounded again. This time they came from every direction: from the right, left, above and below. Not only voices, but shouts, screams, groans and queer distorted noises, not human in sound. Instinctively, Pratt's hand swept to his sword. But as the Moglu continued to advance, paying no attention to the voices and sounds, Pratt's hand fell away from the sword hilt.

The sounds died away. The voices fell silent. And that was worse than when there had been sound. For now there was only silence in answer to their footsteps. A silence which was more unnerving than all the sounds put together. It was like a mantle of evil, which had fallen about them. Like the darkness, it held a strange power. The power of conveying a mood. And the mood was of compelling fear. Not fear of the known. But of the unknown. It was so palpable that Pratt found himself clenching his fists, gritting his teeth.

Then a single voice, Stentorian shouted:

"Hold!"

"Wait here," one of the giants said in a low voice.

They did as he bid.

Pratt's jaw went slack, when he saw what was approaching. He had expected any number of things. Remembering the four armed Rollers he had first encountered, he thought that the Jannsi were some sort of strange beings, perhaps with more than one head, or possessing a plurality of noses. But what he saw coming toward them was—ridiculous!

The Jannsi were midgets!

They came running from the hives of their pueblos, like ants on the quest for honey. In a moment Pratt and his friends were surrounded by hundreds of them. One, who seemed to be the leader, took command of the situation.

"Enough!" he halted their jabbering. "Let us to council with these."

THE LITTLE men surrounded them and marched in a body to the largest of the low, stone dwellings.

Pratt found time to admire the architectural perfection of their homes. They showed evidence of a high cultural plane, far higher than any of the others he had seen hitherto. More, a closer view of the exteriors showed that they had been constructed cleverly, proving an engineering skill beyond any of the other tribes on Luona.

Although the Jannsi were midgets their homes were almost full scale in their furnishings. Most of the Jannsi stayed outside. When Pratt counted noses he saw that only ten of the little men were on the council. And saw them clearly for the first time, in the lighted interior of the council chamber.

About four feet in height on an average, they had the most enormous head Pratt had ever seen on a human. And the heads were completely bald. Other than their shortness of height and bareness of scalp, they showed no other variations from the usual human form.

"Moglu!" began the leader of the Jannsi in a stern voice. "Give us the reason for this trespass!"

The giants looked at each other for a second. One of them gulped audibly and began:

"It was not of our doing, highness. This man, my master..."

"Your—what!" the midget fairly screamed.

Pratt watched in astonishment as the giant fairly groveled at the Jannsi's exclamation.

"The law...the law, highness. He won me in combat."

"Go on," said the other as the giant hesitated in an apparent waiting for the Jannsi's approval.

"Just a moment!" Pratt decided it was high time he took over. "What is this all about? Who are you? What the hell are you yelling for?"

The bald head, immense as a huge cantaloupe and of about the same color, turned a bright pink. Oddly enough, the midget's face did not change color. It was this that made Pratt burst into uproarious laughter. Midgets and giants, mental telepathy and stupidity, crudity and culture, all together as on the Earth. Only on the moon, there was more of the sideshow atmosphere, what with four-armed men, and armored knights vying with advanced philosophy. It was to laugh, that these huge carcasses of flesh should be afraid of these little men. Why, with a sweep of the hand they could make mince meat of the Jannsi. *Then why—Pratt suddenly wanted to know—did he feel this fear that had so compellingly swept over his senses?*

Suddenly the little men no longer looked like comic valentines. Instead they had become enveloped in an aura of incarnate evil. He noticed their eyes, hidden under flesh, hairless lids, were unblinking in their intense surveyal of him. The leader in particular kept his eyes glued to his face with a stare almost hypnotic. Then, like a flash from the blue, strange words impinged on his mind. They were strange only in that they were so unexpected:

"Watch! Be careful! They are experts in hypnotism!"

He had no need of searching for the one who sent the message. Only the Moglu had the means of sending it. Automatically, he re-acted as the giant wanted him to. And not a moment too soon.

Thought waves winged their way to him. They came from all sides.

"Look at us!"

"DO NOT BE AFRAID!"

"WE ARE YOUR FRIENDS!"

He thought it funny that these commands should be capitalized, as if they had come to him on a tape.

SUMMONING all his will power, he closed his mind to everything he heard with it. *"Only the extraneous matters,"* he willed fiercely.

Suddenly there was a void in the air, which in the moment before had been filled with the clash of dynamic personalities. A voice, low, mute with power, intruded into the silence:

"What do you want here?"

It was the leader of these strange little beings.

Pratt could not take the chance of thinking. He acted with instinct. Shrugging his shoulders, he said:

"I don't know. We were brought here by the Moglu."

The huge-headed little man turned his gaze to the giants.

"Why did you bring them here?"

"The short one—his father is Komu of the Stammats— they heard of the Hammar invasion," one of the giants stuttered.

"They compelled us to accompany them," bleated the other.

"Why did you bring them here, fools?" asked the inexorable voice.

"We thought that you could deal more properly with them," came the answer.

The leader of the Jannsi was silent for a moment in introspection. The same blank look was on his face when he said, at last:

"Good! You were wise in bringing them here."

"Yeah. Why?" Pratt wanted to know.

"Because," the little man with the big head said in reply, "there are certain things which are not to be divulged—until we want them to be."

"And suppose we don't feel like staying?"

"That too has been taken into account."

Pratt smiled shallowly. There were a lot of them, it was true. But he had an idea that they were too smart to fight. There must be another reason for their seeming indifference. Still, he had to know. Drawing his sword, Pratt began a slow retreat, drawing Laeri with him, with his free arm.

"Behind you," came a sudden warning to his brain.

He whirled with the speed of light.

Just in time to leap from the path of a sword blade's slicing sweep. His leap carried him half way across the room, backward, over the table in the center. His feet had barely touched the ground then he had jumped once more, back into the fray. Too late to save Laeri, but not too late to avenge him.

The room had suddenly filled with armed men. Strangers. Normal sized men. He had seen one of them strike Laeri and saw Maeri's brother go down. Blind, all-consuming rage swept over him at the sight. He landed among them, his sword lashing at them in powerful blows. *Chips fell from them as his sword struck.*

He had been more or less aware that they were dressed differently than the Jannsi. But it was a momentary glimpse. Now he saw them for what they were, the stone men of the cave. He went cold in a numb sort of horror at the realization. That such a thing could be. That they could move...and talk. For of a sudden he saw one open his mouth...and words came out: slow hesitant words, as though the act of talking was a task just learned:

"Kill! Kill! Must kill!"

IT WAS IN that numb second, when his faculties were in the grip of this new horror, that the Jannsi chief struck with the weapon of hypnotism. Pratt felt as if he had been struck an actual physical blow, it affected him so. Not alone was his mind petrified but so were all his physical properties. He had been in a crouch at the moment of recognition. When he tried to straighten, he couldn't.

He felt the message the Jannsi brain sent to one of the stone men:

"Strike now!"

But there was nothing he could do about it. He saw the stone arm rise above the carved head, saw the sword it held descend in an incredibly slow movement, and felt it strike— and knew no more.

"IF THE Master will permit."

Pratt heard the words as from a vast distance. And heard someone answer:

"Aye!"

"It is only too apparent that our plans for the conquest of Luona have been circulated over the planet. We have looked into the mind of the Earthman and found in the memory lobe of his brain the impressions of past conversations with Komu and his Haifa. Further, we have found..."

"Spare us, Lister. We all know the results."

"...Well then. I think that the time to strike is now! If they should discover the Cavern of the Stone Men—and guess correctly the reason for them, it would be a simple matter to seal it."

The second voice answered in a bored tone:

"All that has been provided for, Lister. As for our plan, it will be put into execution soon. The Moglu will return to Komu, bearing news of his son's capture. They will volunteer or rather leap at the chance to come to his rescue. For there will be an added incentive: the Moglu will tell them that they escaped and can lead them to us. Therefore they will bring their entire army or armies to the field."

"They?" the second voice interrupted.

The first voice held a hint of sarcasm when it replied to the question:

"Have you forgotten that one of the principal points in out plan was to bring all enemies of our people together in one place so that it will be the easier to execute them? And what better place than the field of battle? Especially when it be of our choosing!"

There was an interval of silence. An interval in which Pratt was in turn tortured by what he heard and by the visions brought to his mind of the consequences. Maeri! The thought of her and her gentle loveliness at the mercy of the Jannsi made him see red. He had not the slightest doubt that what they meant by the taking of the women would lead to some form of artificial insemination. He strained his will power to the utmost. But it was of no use. They had placed him under bonds beyond breaking.

"Moglu!" the first voice called a command. "You will carry these two to the cavern where lie the rest of the stone men. Deposit them among the rest. Then do as we have instructed you."

The hairy, ape-like face of one of the giant's swam into the ken of Pratt's vision. There was nothing in the giant's face that could be read one way or another. It was blank. Suddenly he was erect. He had a full view of what was in front of him. But beyond that he could see nothing. He could not so much as blink his eyelids. As though it was a magic lantern slide, the body of the other giant appeared carrying a stiffened figure. Pratt recognized the figure immediately. It was Laeri.

Then Pratt knew what they had done to him and Maeri's brother. Somehow or other they had transformed them into stone men. There was no difference in Laeri and all the rest they had seen in the cavern. But if that was so, how was it that he was able to see and hear'? It was all too apparent that Laeri's eyes were stone sightless orbs. Then it was obvious that so were his.

CHAPTER FOURTEEN

THE GIANT placed the stone figure on the floor. Pratt needed no more proof than the solid thump of it hitting against the floor.

He felt himself lifted; felt himself being carried; but when he was placed beside Laeri he had no feeling of the floor. Evidently only some of senses had an awareness of things.

Then the Jannsi gave the two giants their last order:

"Be off, then, and do not delay more than necessary."

They were escorted by the midgets until they reached the limits of the shallow circular valley in which was located the village, but it wasn't until the giants had placed them in the narrow gutter, which ran the length of the truck.

The darkness had given way to a grayness even more depressing than the somnolent gloom usual in the land of the Jannsi. Pratt was, for the first time assailed by the deepest feeling of frustration. It all seemed so useless to him, if there was a purpose in his being transposed to the moon. The adventures leading up to his being taken prisoner by the little men had a comic opera air about them. The direct simplicity of the people he had met were now submerged in the more abstract but more real villainy of the Jannsi. And he realized, too, that his friends, for so he thought of them, were in a position of danger beyond anything in their comprehension. What made it the more horrible was their and his inability to cope with the situation.

The giant who had laid him in the gutter had placed him on his side. He saw in a dim sort of fashion, that they were moving. He heard grating sound of meshing gears and rubber tires soughing on the silicate of the road. He was thankful that his condition was such that he could not feel the bumps. It was small consolation.

The Moglu lifted the two who had a short time before been flesh and blood, and carried them into the cavern. When they arrived in the hall in which the rest of the petrified men stood in their orderly rows of muse waiting, they stood Pratt and Laeri among them. They stepped back and looked at them. Pratt wondered at their looks of worried introspection. They had done their traitorous work well. He was dumbfounded, when he heard one of them say:

"And now that we have found the reason for these, what can we do about it?"

"Yes," said the other. "What? The Earthman is now as the rest. We were fools! What avail were their armor and weapons against the insidious minds of the Little Men?"

"But what else were we to do, brother?" the other wailed. "The Earthman has the strength of ten. He would have killed us had we not led him to the Jannsi."

"Why," burst out the first, "why must the giant and the midget have the greatest intelligence on this planet? The rest, like children, have the capacity only for games. Would it have availed us anything to have warned them that we knew the Jannsi were plotting the slavery of a whole planet? They would only have—bah! And when we did find someone who might have the drive and courage to circumvent these evil things, he had to carry with him a well-developed sense of suspicion. Now he is as the rest! And we are the worst off for it."

"Exactly! For now, after centuries of planning they are ready to strike, we who were the only ones to know of their desires, can do nothing. Always, we thought it was through hypnotism that they enslaved. Now we know that they have a machine that does it. And when the moment comes, these beings in here will march forth in their invulnerable, stone cloaks. And who will stand against them?"

They sighed in unison. Then the first said:

"What I don't understand, is why they have to march at all? Why, with this machine they could enslave all of us."

"I thought of that," said the other. "And I can only assume that it has a limited range. Remember, brother, that they placed our friends under its influence, one at a time."

"I think you are right. And each had to be given his instruction at the time he was under the machine."

"And what a simple yet effective instruction it was. 'Strike the enemy when we order you to.'"

Once more they heaved simultaneous sighs.

"Well," said one after a moment, "we might as well leave. As little good as our warning will do, we must warn them nevertheless."

The other nodded in agreement. They took a last hopeless look at Pratt and Laeri and left.

PRATT'S darkest suspicions were confirmed. Still he felt a glow of satisfaction in the thought that he had been wrong about the Moglu. They were his and the rest of the planet's friends. Not that it was going to do anyone good. He was almost thankful that the Jannsi had only bound his body. Although his thoughts were on the dark side, he at least was free to think. And not being pessimistic by nature, he felt that there had to be some way out of their dilemma. He thought again of what the two giants had said. Nothing there. The Jannsi controlled their bodily movements. What were the words the Moglu had said they used? "Strike the enemy when we order you to." And of course the enemy was to be whoever confronted them. Whoever—confronted—them! If Pratt had the power to smile just then, it would have reached from ear to ear.

He became aware of a tingling sensation. It started down low, somewhere in the region of his feet and spread upward, until his whole body was an itching, tingling mass. It felt very much like when a member of his body had fallen asleep and the blood had started to circulate once again. The tingling became almost unbearable and he sub-consciously started to lift his hand to scratch. To his complete surprise he was able to complete the gesture. It wasn't, however, a natural gesture. Rather it was something like an automaton would move his arm. There was that same stiffness of movement.

Then he became aware of movement other than his. He turned his head, and in the act was once more surprised that he was able to do so, and saw that Laeri was also lifting his arm to scratch. More, every figure in the hall was doing the same thing. It was the silliest thing he ever saw.

He noticed then, that the tingling sensation had stopped and another desire had taken place. Almost as soon as he was aware of the new desire his mind had translated it into action. His hand had fallen down to where his sword lay sheathed. And had pulled it from its stone receptacle. He realized what was taking place when he saw that the rest were doing the same thing. A train of action had been put into being by a previously given command. Post hypnotism in fact.

The first file of men nearest the cave entrance turned in that direction as one man and marched forward, the rest wheeling in order to follow. As much as Pratt willed for his body to disobey the mental order, he found it of no avail. Like the rest he wheeled when his row's turn came and marched with them to the cave's entrance.

There were several hundred men lined up before the hill when he got there. Automatically, he walked forward to his place in the line. In a matter of minutes the whole of the army which had been within were lined up outside. Once again he felt the tingling sensation. It always seemed to presage any physical movement. For immediately afterward the first rank moved forward.

An army of stone men on the march. An army invulnerable to any of the weapons which could be set against them. An army that had received its orders and was powerless to disobey them!

Pratt felt no discomfort. In fact, he felt nothing. The fine sand made a pleasant crunching sound beneath his stone feet. He turned his head and observed the long ranks of men behind him, the long rows of automatons, marching four abreast. It was an awe-inspiring sight. And fear compelling. For if his plan would not work? He put the thought from him. It was too frightening.

The road took the last turn before they reached the plain leading into Stamat. Already the first few ranks had passed from view. Then his row had made the turn and they were on the level grassy plain. And Pratt saw that the Moglu had done a good job of convincing Laeri's father of the danger Luona faced. For drawn up in a huge semi-circle was the entire armies of all of Komu's allies.

It was an impressive sight!

THERE were several thousand men, some mounted but most on foot. It was broad daylight and the sun reflected from the shining swords and spears they carried. In the very front rank were the armored men of Jama-at's command. Pratt heard the vast roar of shouted defiance, which came from the thousands of throats when they saw the petrified enemy. But there was no answering sound from those who were coming to oppose them. Only silence. But in that silence was a threat greater than any words could describe.

Pratt and the rest continued to march forward until they were in the very heart of the semi-circle. Until they were entirely surrounded by a gleaming steel horn. When the last of them had come into the encompassing prongs, the prongs drew close together until it became a circle. Then a mounted figure rose in his saddle and waving his sword in the direction of the enemy, shouted:

"Charge!"

Simultaneously, there was projected on Pratt's mind the word images that had been placed there by the Jannsi, "strike the enemy!" *And Pratt knelt and picked up a rock at his feet and hurled it into the face of the man directly behind him.* He only waited until he saw the rock strike, then he stooped once more and picked up another. This one he heaved deep into the ranks of stone men.

Indescribable confusion reigned in a matter of seconds. For the one who had been struck first had retaliated by heaving a rock at Pratt. But his aim was not as good as the Earthman's. For the rock struck someone beyond Pratt. That one in turn seeing the missile, also stooped and found a rock and also heaved it. Forgotten were the swords they carried on their shoulders. They had been commanded to strike the enemy. But they had not been told with what.

Pratt had hurled a rock and in turn had one hurled at him. It was an imitation like an animal's the way the entire army stooped to find stone missiles.

And then the mounted men struck among them. For a moment, it almost proved to be the wrong move. For the stone men immediately turned against them. Pratt realized that something had to be done before it was too late. Lifting his sword, he brought it down with all his strength on the shoulder of the man nearest him. A large crack appeared in the stone of the man's body. Pratt did not wait to see the effect of the blow. Movement had been restored to him. Although he could not get around as quickly as when he was flesh and blood, he did have a certain amount of freedom of movement. Enough for what he wanted to do.

He leaped among the automatons, striking as he went. Nor did he try to kill. He was content just to strike a blow and leap away. It was enough. It appeared as though their minds were also petrified, for none seemed to know who did the striking. Nor did they care. A blow had been struck them and they knew only to retaliate. And whoever was nearest became the recipient.

Not all of them, however, fought against each other. There were some who fought against the flesh and blood warriors attacking them. And against those, the legions of Komu and his friends made no headway. For the spears broke against the impregnable stone and the swords were likewise shattered. Nor was the armor in which Komu's own men were clothed sufficient protection against the stone swords of the petrified men.

Pratt made his way to where the Stamat chieftain and Jama-at were unavailingly hacking at the animated statues.

"Komu!" he shouted.

His voice was heard above the sound of clashing arms.

"It is I, the Earthman. Order your forces to retreat!"

THE TWO stepped back in amazement at the sight of him. It was obvious to him that they did not recognize him. Instead of doing as he said, they stepped warily forward. In their careful advance, Pratt read their unwillingness to commit themselves to a course any more perilous than of their own choosing. To them, he was another of the monstrous figures who had to be destroyed. Worse, for since they did not recognize him, they could have but a single purpose in the way they approached. To kill him. He stood his ground, even though he knew it was hopeless to attempt another appeal. From the corner of his eye, he saw more of the Stamat tribesmen follow their chief in his advance. As for the stone men, it made no difference to them. Not having any adversaries of flesh, they fought among themselves. Pratt was in a dilemma from which there seemed no escape. Then a voice, hoarse, thundering in warning:

"Hold!"

It was one of the giants.

"Hold!" he shouted once again. "It *is* the Earthman! I recognize him."

They stopped dead in their tracks at the Moglu's warning. There was utter disbelief to be seen in the eyes of the two and those who were following. Then Jama-at took his courage in hand and stepped warily forward until he was face to face with Pratt.

"It is as the Moglu says," he shouted joyously.

Instantly, Pratt was surrounded by the Stamat men.

"My son? Where is he?" Komu asked. There was fear in his voice.

Quickly Pratt spoke his mind.

"Call off your men! Have them throw rocks and spears among the stone men. They have no minds and will seek the nearest one on which to avenge themselves. I will find Laeri."

He did not wait to see what the reception was to his words but turned and made his way as quickly as he could to where he had last seen Laeri.

It was a wild and confused melee into which he committed himself. The Jannsi had enslaved the minds of these men when they were alive. But now they were dead. As dead as if literally so. Somehow they had managed to retain the last command given them by the evil midgets. But their reasoning power was gone. They acted with a perverted sort of instinct. Pratt, on seeing the purely automatic reactions they had back in the cave, knew that his plan had a good chance of succeeding. And his plan was a simple one. He had remembered the story of Jason and the dragon's teeth. It had and was still working.

If he could only reach Laeri before they destroyed both him and Komu's son!

He knew his task was no easy one. They were almost all dressed alike. But he had not remembered seeing any others who wore armor. So Laeri, then, should be the only one wearing stone armor. It was a tedious as well as dangerous job. For the armor he wore being as fine as silk in the way it clung to the body's contours, folded around the figure and made it necessary for Pratt to examine closely each one he approached.

Time after time he was attacked. Time after time he barely warded off the clumsy attempts on his life. Then he saw a knot of them locked in close embrace. Their swords had been thrown aside and they were striking each other with their fists. He started to pass them when his keen eyes saw the peculiarly shaped hood of Laeri's headpiece.

CHAPTER FIFTEEN

LIFTING HIS sword high above his head Pratt leaped into the fray. The stone weapon came down across the shoulders of the nearest man—and broke in two, so powerful was the blow. And Pratt saw the sun reflect from the steel core in the broken piece that lay on the ground. Some of the mystery was gone. He knew, at least, that the Jannsi coated these people with a solution of something that gave them a petrified coating, but left them as they were on the inside. And realized too the horror of the situation. For if the steel still remained in the sword, then the flesh still remained in the body. So that when one of their members was whacked off, the living flesh went with it also. He saw the proof of that in the arm that had been hacked off by his sword. He could see the bones, tendons, fat in its neat layers where the arm had been joined to the shoulder. The moment of stunned surprise almost cost his life. And taught him something else.

First that there was no physical sensation attached to the act. For the stone man didn't even turn to look at the wound. And in that instant the stone man reached him, Pratt had time only to throw up a protecting arm against the blow that was dealt him. He heard a crack and felt his heart turn in sick protest in fear of what it might mean. But it wasn't his arm. It was the others.

Pratt leaped back and the other continued after him. Pratt didn't know what to do. Caution bade him retreat. If he did Laeri's chances for revival were practically nil. Somehow, whether it was because there was something different in the physical makeups of the peoples of the moon and earth, or whatever it was, but the effects of what the Janna, had done acted differently on Pratt. Mentally he was as alert as ever. But in that he was alone. So Laeri's reactions were as the rest. And in that was his biggest danger. For even if Pratt did reach him in time, there was the chance that Laeri would turn on him.

Suddenly Pratt felt an overpowering sensation of anger against these dumb Frankenstein-like monsters. Lowering his head he charged, football-fashion, into the heap of stone bodies. Disregarding any risk that he might be taking, he bulled his way to the center of the pile by sheer strength. His fists flailed a path before him. It was a miracle that he was all in one piece by the time he reached Laeri. The same could not be said for most of those who were unfortunate enough to have got into the way of those hammering fists. Broken members of bodies strewed the path he hacked out.

Laeri, like the rest, was engaged in a senseless pounding at whatever was in front of him. Pratt whirled him around and threw him over his shoulder. There had been perhaps fifteen of the stone men in path when he started to Laeri. There were still seven who were whole. Some latent sense of anger made them draw together in mutual bond to oppose him. A single glance told him that there was little chance of either surviving the gamut they were being forced to run.

ONCE AGAIN he closed his mind to the danger. They were drawn about him in a loose semi-circle. Pratt started toward the center of the group, then as those to the top of the center swung to meet him, he shifted to the other end, running at full speed as he did so. Encumbered as he was, his speed was still too great for them to intercept. He struck the only one left to oppose him a tremendous blow and caromed off. The one who was struck simply disintegrated. Stone pieces flew in every direction.

Regaining his balance, Pratt continued to run until he was beyond pursuit. Then he placed the squirming body of Laeri on the ground.

"Well," he said softly, "you're safe at last."

The sightless eyes of Maeri's brother regarded him dispassionately for a second. Then, before Pratt could prevent or escape, Laeri brought his arm down on Pratt's head. There was a rushing sound, as of waters breaking loose. Darkness, interspersed with pinpoints of light became for an instant all of Pratt's life. Then there was only darkness.

FIRST THERE was stillness. Not the stillness of unconsciousness, but the quiet of a room that has no occupant. Then there was the sound of a door opening. The rustle of sandaled feet. The warmth of a body bending over his bed. Then the press of soft lips on his in a gentle caress.

Pratt sighed and Maeri drew back. He opened his eyes and saw her regarding him with eyes that were wide and filled to overflowing with love. Tears wormed their way to the corners when she saw that he was awake. He lifted his arms and she flew into them with a keening sound.

"Darling," she moaned. "My dear! You will be well."

He looked at his arms. They were still stone clad. The tiny hope he held that he was as he had been, died.

"How long...how long," he began again, "was I unconscious?"

"Since yesterday."

"And Laeri? Where is he?"

Her face clouded over at the words.

She gulped and her words came hard:

"They...had to bind him tightly so that he could harm no one."

"Where is your father?" Pratt asked.

"In the great hall."

Pratt swung his legs over the side of the bed. She drew back in alarm. "You feel well enough?" she asked breathlessly.

He nodded and stood erect. There were no ill effects attached to the blow he had received. He stretched his arms above his head and bent at the knees.

"Good as new," he said to the girl who was regarding him with puzzled glance. "Well, might as well complete my unfinished business."

"What do you mean?"

"Those little men," he answered and his voice was suddenly tight. "They need to be taught a lesson—in morals. On Earth we have certain moral precepts. Covet not thy neighbors goods is one of them. They broke that. And so…" he did not need to complete his sentence. She understood.

Once again she pressed her lips to his cold stone ones. He thought it odd that he could feel their warmth. He patted her shoulder gently and left.

His footsteps made a thunderous sound as he came into the now familiar hall. It was as if he had just left. The same men were gathered about the huge table. Only Laeri was missing. Every face turned in his direction. And fifty voices roared a welcome. He nodded gravely to them. They waited, expectant and hushed for his words. And each felt that what he was going to say was going to effect each of them to the greatest degree.

He looked about him. Into every face. And was heartened by what he saw. For in each face was the same grim determination. They would follow wherever he led.

"The vehicle," he said to the two giants who were standing to one side, "you have it here?"

"Aye, Master."

"Good! We will have need of it."

"What are your intentions?" Jama-at asked.

"Those little men," Pratt answered coldly, "must be destroyed. Each and every one of them. I don't think I'm wrong when I say that any attack by the means you possess will do any good. The stone men are immune to your weapons. But in that truck is a weapon that none of them can withstand. And all the men I'll need will be the Moglu."

"You mean," Komu broke in, in a somewhat querulous tone, "that you won't need us?"

Pratt nodded gravely.

Komu's face showed his disappointment.

"If I don't succeed," Pratt said in grim reminder, "you will have your fill of fighting. I don't think that they will stop with that first attack. From what I overheard, they want what you possess very much."

Komu sighed heavily and turned to look into each face around the table. Satisfied with what he saw, he turned to Pratt and said:

"Very well, Earthman. Go with our hopes and blessings. We will follow. And if you do not succeed, then…"

Once more Pratt nodded. Then gesturing for the giants to follow, he strode from the room.

THE TRUCK rode with its familiar smoothness. Pratt felt slightly uncomfortable. His body was not as limber in the state it was in as when it was of flesh. One of the giants rode in his seat behind the cabin. The other was driving. The Earth, which had illuminated their ride for the most part, had already disappeared. The half-darkness of the land was enveloping them. The Jannsi stronghold was not far off.

Pratt asked what had been on his mind ever since he had heard the Moglu discuss the situation back in the cave:

"Tell me," he asked, "why didn't you warn the people what the Jannsi were planning?"

The giant turned and regarded him soberly. Shaking his head, he answered:

"It would have done no good. In the first place, we didn't know exactly what they were planning. We knew of the cave and brought you to it deliberately to hear your reaction to what was within. As a matter of fact, my brother and I had brought many of them into that hiding place. And that is not the only one. They have two more such. But to get back to you, we thought or rather hoped that somehow you would find the way to circumvent them. As it turned out we were wrong. We forgot that you were susceptible to hypnotism.

"Then, when we finally learned what was behind the whole thing, it was too late. For even if we warned Komu and his allies, the fact that the Jannsi held you and Laeri captive would make them regard us and our motives with suspicion. Therefore, we decided simply to say that you had been taken prisoner and take our chances that the battle would resolve in our favor."

"Well," Pratt said grimly. "if my plan goes through, we can stop worrying about those jerks. And I hope that they have all their petrified friends with them when we get there."

The giant had an idea of Pratt's intention. But since he would not elaborate on his thoughts, the giant kept his peace. Then they were before the shallow, circular valley of the Jannsi. The Moglu braked the truck to a gentle and silent step. There was a difference in the appearance of the place this time. The whole valley was aglow with light, light in the torches held by thousands of the petrified warriors. The whole valley was filled with them. And they could see that the small houses of the Jannsi had been transformed into beehives of industry. The little men kept running in and out like ants.

"Not a moment too soon," Pratt said. "I've an idea that they're getting ready to move. All right. Here's what I want you to do. Remember what we did to the village of At-tu? I checked the gauge back at Stamat and we have a little better than twenty thousand gallons left. Your brother and I'll hold the hoses and let the gas drain out while you drive. Go like hell! We've got to circle the whole damned valley."

THEN, WHILE the giant drove, Pratt and the other Moglu let the precious gas drain. Pratt's heart stayed in his mouth all through the tortuous trip. A single spark could set the gasoline aflame prematurely and provide a flaming, horrible coffin for them. The stench of it was overpowering. Already the Jannsi had noticed the odor and had come out to investigate. By that time, they had made a complete circuit of the valley.

Pratt leaped from the truck. The two giants gathered about him. His grin was a terrible thing as he looked at the gas soaked valley. Then it faded from his lips as he realized that all his planning would go for naught. The matches he had intended to use were in one of his pants pockets. And they were encased by an impregnable stone garment. There was only one other means in which he could get the gas to explode.

"Wait here for me!" he commanded, as he got back into the cab.

He switched on the motor and putting it into gear, stepped on the gas. Nothing happened. Once more he stepped on the gas. Nothing happened. And he realized that with a truckload of gas, he had forgotten to put any into the tank. And there was no way of getting any in even if he had any left in the truck.

There was a single way left for him. The slope of the valley was its steepest at this point. The stone ramparts of the Jannsi were only a hundred yards off. If he could get the truck to roll that far and it would strike against the house there was bound to be at least a spark. Perhaps enough to set off an explosion. He stuck his head out of the cab and shouted:

"Push the truck down into the valley!"

It took only a moment. The giants' strength was immense. And coupled with the emergency of the situation, it was more than enough. The truck began to roll, gathering speed as the slope increased. Gasoline splashed in waves from the hose-draped radiator, as though it were the prow of a boat.

Then he was on the first rank of stone men—and through them. They were in ranks ten deep. But it was as if they were ten pins before the bowling ball of the truck. Pratt offered up a prayer of thankfulness that it was not a passenger car he was in. The very weight of the truck was sufficient to carry it through.

There was no time for thinking, then. The dwelling of the Jannsi looked ahead. Pratt twisted the wheel over until the truck was heading straight for it—and leaped from the cab. He was running as fast as he could toward the safety of the valley rim even before the truck struck.

NEVER IN all his life did Pratt ever imagine such a burst of sound could be possible. The very earth quaked from the explosion. A solid sheet of flame leaped sky high when the truck struck. And instantly the whole valley became a sea of flame.

Events moved with all the rapidity of a fast motion picture and all his impressions were viewed as through a kaleidoscope. Suddenly, he had become lighter. His leaps were higher, farther. And as he passed and jumped the men of stone, he was horrified to discover that they were shedding their casings. So with the sound of the holocaust there was added that of men screaming in maddening pain. They were torches running madly about. And futilely, for there was no escape.

Pain swept over Pratt. Excruciating pain! And he saw that where his feet landed and nowhere was there an escape from it, was a lake of fire, several feet deep. The armor he wore was a protecting factor for a few seconds. Then the intense heat became felt in a horrible fashion. It was as if he was encased in a furnace.

Madly, with all the remaining strength of his will and body he leaped in huge strides for the rim of the valley. Fire fell from him at every step. His mind whirled and seemed to shrivel in the cap of his skull. The pain grew unendurable. Worse, he became afraid to breathe. Then he saw the figures of the two giants, tense in waiting, watching with bated breath his race with death. Summoning the last ounce of strength, he reached the top with a great bound, a bound that seemed to burst the blood vessels in his throat. He struck heavily, rolled once or twice and lay still.

CHAPTER SIXTEEN

TELL ME," Maeri said. "Now that the Jannsi have been wiped out, what are you going to do?"

Pratt, looking like a well-wrapped mummy, slid his arm carefully around her waist. He winced slightly. Hearing the sound, she asked in concern:

"Does it still hurt?"

"Honey," he said, laughter in his voice. "When I've got my arm around you, nothing bothers me…except you."

The girl smiled shyly and looked up at the great ball of the Earth, floating in the empyrean reaches of the heavens. He followed her glance and for a moment became speculative. It was the strangest adventure—the most *unbelievable* adventure—that could ever have happened. There floating in space was all that he knew of home. Upon that planet were associations that were part of his…what? They seemed so meaningless now. They were meaningless! This and only this was real. This girl! Those giants who had beat out with their bare hands the flames in which he was wrapped. Who had carried him in their arms as if he were a baby and with as much care, until they reached Stamat and the unguent which saved his life.

He looked at the Earth and knew that he would never go back there. He blinked his eyes rapidly. The Earth...it seemed to be growing in size. It was! The girl's voice seemed to come from a vast distance.

"Darling! What's wrong?"

There was no time to be lost. Wordlessly, he whirled her back into the room.

"Nothing, baby," he answered shakily. "Nothing anymore. Not since I've found you. Tell me honey, do you think your father could use a good truck driver? That is if he had a truck?"

She retreated from him for a few steps. Then he had her close once more and closed off any more questions, by pressing his lips firmly but gently on hers. It was to prove the most effective way of stopping her questions.

THE END

If you've enjoyed this book, you will not want to miss these terrific titles…

ARMCHAIR SCI-FI & HORROR DOUBLE NOVELS, $12.95 each

D-71   **THE DEEP END** by Gregory Luce
TO WATCH BY NIGHT by Robert Moore Williams

D-72   **SWORDSMAN OF LOST TERRA** by Poul Anderson
PLANET OF GHOSTS by David V. Reed

D-73   **MOON OF BATTLE** by J. J. Allerton
THE MUTANT WEAPON by Murray Leinster

D-74   **OLD SPACEMEN NEVER DIE!** John Jakes
RETURN TO EARTH by Bryan Berry

D-75   **THE THING FROM UNDERNEATH** by Milton Lesser
OPERATION INTERSTELLAR by George O. Smith

D-76   **THE BURNING WORLD** by Algis Budrys
FOREVER IS TOO LONG by Chester S. Geier

D-77   **THE COSMIC JUNKMAN** by Rog Phillips
THE ULTIMATE WEAPON by John W. Campbell

D-78   **THE TIES OF EARTH** by James H. Schmitz
CUE FOR QUIET by Thomas L. Sherred

D-79   **SECRET OF THE MARTIANS** by Paul W. Fairman
THE VARIABLE MAN by Philip K. Dick

D-80   **THE GREEN GIRL** by Jack Williamson
THE ROBOT PERIL by Don Wilcox

ARMCHAIR SCIENCE FICTION CLASSICS, $12.95 each

C-25   **THE STAR KINGS**
by Edmond Hamilton

C-26   **NOT IN SOLITUDE**
by Kenneth Gantz

C-32   **PROMETHEUS II**
by S. J. Byrne

ARMCHAIR SCIENCE FICTION & HORROR GEMS SERIES, $12.95 each

G-7   **SCIENCE FICTION GEMS, Vol. Seven**
Jack Sharkey and others

G-8   **HORROR GEMS, Vol. Eight**
Seabury Quinn and others

THE SPACE DOCTOR'S DILEMMA...

The only links between the far-flung colonies throughout the galaxy were the Medical Service spaceships. It was natural therefore that when these lonely travelers paid a call, they were given a royal welcome.

No wonder Med Serviceman Calhoun got the shock of his life when the landing grid on newly colonized Maris III tried to destroy his ship!

And when he managed to make a crash-landing, he was even more shocked by the grisly fact that most of the colonists had starved to death— even though there was plenty of food around. Forgetting his horror, Calhoun had to move fast to keep the fate of Maris III from being the beginning of the end for all the colonial planets.

CAST OF CHARACTERS

CALHOUN

Usually he got a pretty nice reception when he landed on other planets. He didn't know what to think when someone tried to kill him before he landed!

HELEN JONS

When Calhoun found her she was very close to dying, but she wasn't going to go down without trying to take some of her murderers with her!

KIM WALPOLE

This medical man had stayed behind to find answers—and a cure, because what he didn't know was soon going to kill every one of them!

MURGATROYD

Calhoun's right hand, and cutest pet imaginable. Ready, willing and able to test out a certain food, or mix up an antidote if the situation called for it.

THE MICROBIOLOGIST

An old-timer who'd been stewing with hate for a long, long time. He was very good at what he did—making deadly poisons and killing people off!

THE MUTANT
WEAPON

BY
MURRAY LEINSTER

ARMCHAIR FICTION
PO Box 4369, Medford, Oregon   97501-0168

*For more information about Armchair Books and products, visit our
website at…*

www.armchairfiction.com

Or email us at…

armchairfiction@yahoo.com

CHAPTER ONE

"The probability of unfavorable consequences cannot be zero in any action of common life, but the probability increases by a very high power as a series of actions is lengthened.   The effect of moral considerations, in conduct, may be stated to be a mathematically verifiable reduction in the number of unfavorable possible chance happenings. Of course, whether this process is called the intelligent use of probability, or ethics, or piety, makes no difference in the facts.   It is the method by which unfavorable chance happenings are made least probable. Arbitrary actions such as we call criminal cannot ever be justified by mathematics. For example..."

Probability and Human Conduct—Fitzgerald

CALHOUN lay in his bunk and read Fitzgerald on *Probability and Human Conduct* as the little Med Ship floated in overdrive. In overdrive travel there is nothing to do but pass the time away. Murgatroyd, the *tormal*, slept curled up in a ball in one corner of the small ship's cabin. His tail was meticulously curled about his nose. The ship's lights burned steadily. There were those small random noises which have to be provided to keep a man sane in the dead stillness of a ship traveling at very many times the speed of light. Calhoun turned a page and yawned.

Something stirred somewhere. There was a click, and a taped voice said:

"When the tone sounds, breakout will be five seconds off."

A metronomic clicking, grave and deliberate, resounded in the stillness. Calhoun heaved himself up from the bunk and marked his place in the book. He moved to and seated himself in the control chair and fastened the safety belt. He said:

"Murgatroyd. Hark, hark the lark in Heaven's something-or-other doth sing. Wake up and comb your whiskers. We're getting there."

Murgatroyd opened one eye and saw Calhoun in the pilot's chair. He uncurled himself and padded to a place where there was something to grab hold of. He regarded Calhoun with bright eyes.

"Bong!" said the tape. It counted down. "Five...four...three...two...one..."

It stopped. The ship popped out of overdrive. The sensation was unmistakable. Calhoun's stomach seemed to turn over twice, and he had a sickish feeling of spiraling dizzily in what was somehow a cone. He swallowed. Murgatroyd made gulping noises. Outside, everything changed.

The sun Maris blazed silently in emptiness off to port. The Cetis star-cluster was astern, and the light by which it could be seen had traveled for many years to reach here, though Calhoun had left Med Headquarters only three weeks before. The third planet of Maris swung splendidly in its orbit. Calhoun checked, and nodded in satisfaction. He spoke over his shoulder to Murgatroyd.

"We're here, all right."

"Chee!" shrilled Murgatroyd.

He uncoiled his tail from about a cabinet handle and hopped up to look at the vision screen. What he saw, of course, meant nothing to him. But all *tormals* imitate the actions of human beings, as parrots imitate their speech. He blinked wisely at the screen and turned his eyes to Calhoun.

"It's Maris III," Calhoun told him, "and pretty close. It's a colony of Dettra Two. One city was reported started two Earth years ago. It should just about be colonized now."

"Chee-chee!" shrilled Murgatroyd.

"So get out of the way," commanded Calhoun. "We'll make our approach and I'll tell 'em we're here."

He made a standard approach on interplanetary drive. Naturally, it was a long process. But after some hours he flipped over the call switch and made the usual identification and landing request.

"Med Ship Aesclipus Twenty to ground," he said into the transmitter. "Requesting coordinates for landing. Our mass is fifty tons. Repeat, five-oh tons. Purpose of landing: planetary health inspection."

He relaxed. This job ought to be purest routine. There was a landing grid in the spaceport city on Maris III. From its control room instructions should be sent, indicating a position some five planetary diameters from the surface of that world. Calhoun's little ship should repair to that spot. The giant landing grid should then reach out its specialized force field, lock onto the ship, and bring it gently but irresistibly down to ground. Then Calhoun, representing Med Service, should confer gravely with planetary authorities about public health conditions on Maris III.

It was not to be expected that anything important would turn up. Calhoun would deliver full details of recent advances in the science of medicine. These might already have reached Maris III in the ordinary course of commerce, but he would make sure. He might—but it was unlikely—learn of some novelty worked out here. In any case, within three days he should return to the small Med Ship, the landing grid should heave it firmly heavenward to not less than five planetary diameters distance, and there release it. And Calhoun and Murgatroyd and the Med Ship should flick into overdrive and speed back toward headquarters, from whence they had come.

Right now, Calhoun waited for an answer to his landing call. But he regarded the vast disk of the nearby planet.

"By the map," he observed to Murgatroyd, "the city ought to be on shore of that bay somewhere near the terminus. Close to the sunset line."

His call was answered. A voice said incredulously on the spacephone speaker:

"What? What's that? What's that you say?"

"Med Ship Aesclipus Twenty," Calhoun repeated patiently. "Requesting coordinates for landing. Our mass is fifty tons. Repeat, five-oh tons. Purpose of landing: planetary health inspection."

The voice said more incredulously still:

"A Med Ship? Holy—" By the change of sound, the man down on the planet had turned away from the microphone. *"Hey! Listen to this!"*

There was abrupt silence. Calhoun raised his eyebrows. He drummed on the control desk before him. There was a long pause. A very long pause. Then a new voice came on the spacephone, up from the ground:

"You up there! Identify yourself!"

Calhoun said very politely:

"This is Med Ship Aesclipus Twenty. I would like to come to ground. Purpose of landing: health inspection."

"Wait," said the voice from the planet. It sounded strained.

A murmuring sounded, transmitted from fifty thousand miles away. Then there was a click. The transmitter down below had cut off. Calhoun raised his eyebrows again. This was not according to routine. Not at all! The Med Service was badly overworked and understaffed. The resources of interplanetary services were always apt to be stretched to their utmost, because there could be no galactic government as such. Many thousands of occupied planets, the closest of them light-years apart, couldn't hold elections or have political parties for the simple reason that travel, even in overdrive, was too slow. They could only have service organizations whose authority depended on the consent of the people served, and whose support had to be gathered when and as it was possible.

But the Med Service was admittedly important. The local Sector Headquarters was in the Cetis cluster. It was a sort of interstellar clinic, with additions. It gathered and disseminated the results of experience in health and medicine among some thousands of colony-worlds, and from time to time it made contact with other headquarters carrying on the same work elsewhere. It admittedly took fifty years for a new technique in gene selection to cross the occupied part of the galaxy, but it was a three-year voyage in overdrive to cover the same distance direct. And the Med Service was worthwhile. There was no problem of human ecological adjustment it had so far been unable to solve, and there were some dozens of planets whose human colonies owed their existence to it. There was nowhere, nowhere at all, that a Med Ship was not welcomed on its errand from headquarters.

"Aground there!" said Calhoun sharply. "What's the matter? Are you landing me or not?"

There was no answer. Then, suddenly, every sound-producing device in the ship abruptly emitted a hoarse and monstrous noise. The lights flashed up and circuit breakers cut them off. The nearest-object horn squawked. The hull temperature warning squealed. The ship's internal gravity field tugged horribly for an instant and went off. Every device within the ship designed to notify emergency clanged or shrieked or roared or screamed. There was a momentary bedlam.

It lasted for part of a second only. Then everything stopped. There was no weight within the ship, and there were no lights. There was dead silence, and Murgatroyd made whimpering sounds in the darkness.

Calhoun thought absurdly to himself, *According to the book, this is an unfavorable chance consequence of something or other.* But it was more than an unfavorable chance occurrence. It was an intentional and drastic and possibly a deadly one.

"Somebody's acting up," said Calhoun measuredly, in the blackness. "What the hell's the matter with them?"

He flipped the screen switch to bring back vision of what was outside. The vision screens of a ship are very carefully fused against overload burnouts, because there is nothing in all the cosmos quite as helpless and foredoomed as a ship which is blind in the emptiness of space. But the screens did not light again. They couldn't. The cutouts hadn't worked in time.

Calhoun's scalp crawled. But as his eyes adjusted, he saw the pale fluorescent handles of switches and doors. They hadn't been made fluorescent in expectation of an emergency like this, of course, but they would help a great deal. He knew what had happened. It could only be one thing—a landing-grid field clamped on the fifty-ton Med Ship with the power needed to grasp and land a twenty-thousand-ton liner. At that strength it would paralyze every instrument and blow every cutoff. It could not be accidental. The reception of the news of his identity, the repeated request that he identify himself, and then the demand that he wait... This murderous performance was deliberate.

"Maybe," said Calhoun in the inky-black cabin, "as a Med Ship our arrival is an unfavorable chance consequence of something—and somebody means to keep us from happening. It looks like it."

Murgatroyd whimpered.

"And I think," added Calhoun coldly, "that somebody may need a swift kick in the negative feedback!"

He released himself from the safety belt and dived across the cabin in which there was now no weight at all. In the blackness he opened a cabinet door. What he did inside was customarily done by a man wearing thick insulated gloves, in the landing grid back at headquarters. He threw certain switches which would allow the discharge of the power-storage cells which worked the Med Ship's overdrive. Monstrous quantities of energy were required to put even a fifty-ton ship into overdrive, and monstrous amounts were returned when it came out. The power amounted to ounces of pure, raw energy, and as a safety precaution such amounts were normally put into the Duhanne cells only just before a Med Ship's launching, and drained out again on its return. But now, Calhoun threw switches which made a rather incredible amount of power available for dumping into the landing-grid field about him—if necessary.

He floated back to the control chair.

The ship lurched. Violently. It was being moved by the grid field without any gentleness at all. Calhoun's hands barely grasped the back of his pilot's chair before the jerk came, and it almost tore them free. He just missed being flung against the back of the cabin by the applied acceleration. But he was a long way out from the planet. He was at the end of a lever fifty thousand miles long, and for that lever to be used to shake him too brutally would require special adjustments. But somebody was making them. The jerk reversed directions. He was flung savagely against the chair to which he'd been clinging. He struggled. Another yank, in another direction. Another one still. It flung him violently into the chair.

Behind him, Murgatroyd squealed angrily as he went hurtling across the cabin. He grabbed for holding places with all four paws and his tail.

Another shake. Calhoun had barely fastened the safety belt before a furious jolt nearly flung him out of it again to crash against the cabin ceiling. Still another vicious surge of acceleration, and he scrabbled for the controls. The yanking and plunging of the ship increased intolerably. He was nauseated. Once he was thrust so furiously into the control chair that the was on the verge of blacking out; and then the direction of thrust was changed to the exact opposite so that the blood rushing to his head seemed about to explode it. His arms flailed out of control. He became dazed. But when his hands were flung against the control board, he tried, despite their bruising, to cling to the control-knobs, and each time he threw them over. Practically all his circuits were blown, but there was one—

His numbing fingers threw it. There was a roar so fierce that it seemed to be an explosion. He'd reached the switch which made effective the discharge circuit of his Duhanne cells. He'd thrown it. It was designed to let the little ship's overdrive power reserve flow into storage at headquarters on return from duty. Now, though, it poured into the landing field outside. It amounted to hundreds of millions of kilowatt hours, delivered in the fraction of a second. There was the smell of ozone. The sound was like a thunderclap.

But abruptly there was a strange and incredible peace. The lights came on waveringly as his shaking fingers restored the circuit breakers. Murgatroyd shrilled indignantly, clinging desperately to an instrument rack. But the vision screens did not light again. Calhoun swore. Swiftly, he threw more circuit restorers. The nearest-object indicator told of the presence of Maris III at forty-odd thousand miles. The hull temperature indicator was up some fifty-six degrees. The internal-gravity field came on faintly, and then built up to normal. But the screens would not light. They were permanently dead. Calhoun raged for seconds. Then he got hold of himself.

"Chee-chee-chee!" chattered Murgatroyd desperately. *"Chee-chee!"*

"Shut up!" growled Calhoun. "Some bright lad aground thought up a new way to commit murder. Damned near got away with it, too! He figured he'd shake us to death like a dog does a rat, only he was using a landing-grid field to do it with. Right now, I hope I fried him!"

But it was not likely. Such quantities of power as are used to handle twenty-thousand-ton spaceliners are not controlled direct, but by relays. The power Calhoun had flung into the grid field should have blown out the grid's transformers with a spectacular display of fireworks, but it was hardly probable it had gotten back to the individual at the controls.

"But I suspect," observed Calhoun vengefully, "that he'll consider this business an unfavorable occurrence. Somebody'll twist his tail too, either for trying what he did or for not getting away with it! Only, as a matter of pure precaution—

His expression changed suddenly. He'd been trying not to think of the consequences of having no sight of the cosmos outside the ship. Now he remembered the electron telescope. It had not been in circuit, so it could not have been burned out like his vision screens. He switched it on. A star-field appeared over his head.

"Chee-chee!" cried Murgatroyd hysterically.

Calhoun glanced at him. The jerking of the ship had shifted the instruments in the rack to which Murgatroyd clung. Clipped into place though they were, they'd caught Murgatroyd's tail and pinched it tightly.

"You'll have to wait," snapped Calhoun. "Right now I've got to make us look like a successful accident. Otherwise, whoever tried to spread us all over the cabin walls will try something else!"

The Med Ship flung through space in whatever direction and at whatever velocity it had possessed when the grid field blew. Calhoun shifted the electron-telescope field and simultaneously threw on the emergency rocket controls. There was a growling of the pencil-thin, high-velocity blasts. There was a surging of the ship.

"No straight-line stuff," Calhoun reminded himself.

He swung the ship into a dizzy spiral, as if innumerable things had been torn or battered loose in the ship and its rockets had come on of themselves. Painstakingly, he jettisoned in one explosive burst all the stored waste of his journey which could not be disposed of while in overdrive. To any space-scanning instrument on the ground, it would look like something detonating violently inside the ship.

"Now—"

The planet Marris III swung across the electron telescope's field. It looked hideously near, but that was the telescope's magnification. Yet Calhoun sweated. He looked at the nearest-object dial for reassurance. The planet was nearer by a thousand miles.

"Hah!" said Calhoun.

He changed the ship's spiral course. He changed it again. He abruptly reversed the direction of its turn. Adequate training in space combat could have helped plot an evasion course, but it might have been recognizable. Nobody could anticipate his maneuvers now, though. He adjusted the telescope next time the planet swept across its field, and flipped on the photorecorder. Then he pulled out of the spiral, whirled the ship until the city was covered by the telescope, and ran the recorder as long as he dared keep a straight course. Then he swooped toward the planet in a crazy, twisting fall with erratic intermissions, and made a final lunatic dash almost parallel to the planet's surface.

At five hundred miles he unshielded the ports, which of necessity had to be kept covered in clear space. There was a sky which was vividly bright with stars. There was a vast blackness off to starboard which was the night side of the planet.

He went down. At four hundred miles the outside-pressure indicator wavered away from its pin. He used it like a Pilot-tube recording, doing sums in his head to figure the static pressure that should exist at this height, to compare with the dynamic pressure produced by his velocity through the near hard vacuum. The pressure should have been substantially zero. He swung the ship end-for-end and killed velocity to bring the pressure indication down. The ship descended. Two hundred miles. He saw the thin bright line of sunshine at the limb of the planet. Down to one hundred. He cut the rockets and let the ship fall silently, swinging its nose up.

At ten miles he listened for man-made radiation. There was nothing in the electromagnetic spectrum but the crackling of static in an electric storm which might be a thousand miles away. At five miles height the nearest-object indicator, near the bottom of its scale, wavered in a fashion to prove that he was still moving laterally across mountainous country. He swung the ship and killed that velocity too.

At two miles he used the rockets for deceleration. The pencil-thin flame reached down for an incredible distance. By naked-eye observation out a port, he tilted the fiercely roaring, swiftly falling ship until hillsides and forests underneath him ceased to move. By that time he was very low indeed.

He reached ground on a mountainside which was lighted by the blue-white flame of the rocket blast. He chose an area in which the treetops were almost flat, indicating something like a plateau underneath. Murgatroyd was practically frantic by this time because of his capture and the pinching of his tail, but Calhoun could not spare time to release him. He let the ship down gently, gently, trying to descend in an absolutely vertical line.

If he didn't do it perfectly, he came very close. The ship settled into what was practically a burned-away tunnel among monstrous trees. The slender, high-velocity flame did not splash when it reached ground. It penetrated. It burned a hole for itself through humus and clay and bedrock. When the ship touched and settled, there was boiling molten stone some sixty feet underground; but there was only a small scratching sound as it came to rest. A flame-amputated tree limb rubbed tentatively against the hull.

Calhoun turned off the rockets. The ship swayed slightly and there were crunching noises. Then it was still on its landing fins.

"Now," said Calhoun, "I can take care of you, Murgatroyd."

He flicked on the switches of the exterior microphones, which were much more sensitive than human ears. The radiation detectors were still in action. They reported only the cracklings of the distant storm.

But the microphones brought in the moaning of wind over nearby mountaintops, and the almost deafening susurrus of rustling leaves. Underneath these noises there was a bedlam of other natural sounds. There were chirpings and hootings and squeaks, and the gruntings made by native animal life. These sounds had a singularly peaceful quality. When Calhoun toned them down to be no more than background noise, they suggested the sort of concert of night-creatures which to men has always seemed an indication of purest tranquility.

Presently Calhoun looked at the pictures the photorecorder had taken while the telescope's field swept over the city. It was the colony-city reported to have been begun two years before, to receive colonists from Dettra Two. It was the city of the landing-grid which had tried to destroy the Med Ship as a dog kills a rat, by shaking it to fragments, some forty thousand miles in space. It was the city which had made Calhoun land with his vision plates blinded; which had made him pretend his ship was internally a wreck; which had drained his power reserves of some hundreds of millions of kilowatt-hours of energy. It was the city which had made his return to Med Headquarters impossible.

He inspected the telescopic pictures. They were very clear. They showed the city with astonishing detail. There was a lacy pattern of highways, with their medallions of multiple-dwelling units. There were the lavish park areas between the buildings of this planetary capital. There was the landing grid itself, a half-mile high structure of steel girders, a full mile in diameter.

But there were no vehicles on the highways. There were no specks on the overpasses to indicate people on foot. There were no 'copters on the building roofs, nor were there objects in mid-air to tell of air traffic.

The city was either deserted or it had never been occupied. But it was absolutely intact. The structures were perfect. There was no indication of past panic or disaster, and even the highways had not been overgrown by vegetation. But it was empty—or else it was dead.

But somebody in it had tried very ferociously and with singular effectiveness to try to destroy the Med Ship.

Because it was a Med Ship.

Calhoun raised his eyebrows and looked at Murgatroyd.

"Why is all this?" he asked. "Have you any ideas?"

"Chee!" shrilled Murgatroyd.

CHAPTER TWO

"The purpose of a contemplated human action is always the attainment of a desired subjective experience. But a subjective experience is desired both in terms of intensity and of duration. For an individual the temptingness of different degrees of intensity—of

experience is readily computed. However, the tempting-ness of different durations is equally necessary for an estimate of the probability of a given person performing a given action. This modification of desirability by expected duration depends on the individual's time sense; its acuity and its accuracy. Measurements of time sense..."

Probability and Human Conduct—Fitzgerald

EVENTUALLY Calhoun left the ship and found a culti-vated field and a dead man and other things. But while in the Med Ship he found only bewilderment. The first morning he carefully monitored the entire communications spectrum. There were no man-made signals in the air of Maris III. That was proof the world was uninhabited. But the ship's external microphones picked up a rocket roar in mid-morning. Calhoun looked, and saw the faint white trail of the rocket against the blue of the sky. The fact that he saw it was proof that it was in atmosphere. And that was evidence that the rocket was taking photographs for signs of the crater the Med Ship should have made in a crash landing.

The fact of search was proof that the planet was inhabited, but the silence of the radio spectrum said that it wasn't. The absence of traffic in the city said that it was dead or empty, but there were people there because they'd answered Calhoun's hail, and tried to kill him when he identified himself. But nobody would want to destroy a Med Ship except to prevent a health inspection, and nobody would want to prevent an inspection unless there was a situation aground that the Med Service ought to know about. But there should not be such a situation.

There was no logical explanation for such a series of con-tradictions. Civilized men acted either this way or that. There could only be civilized men here, yet they acted neither this way nor that. Therefore—and the confusion began all over again.

Calhoun dictated an account of events to date into the emergency responder in the ship. If a search call came from space, the responder would broadcast this data and Calhoun's intended action. He carefully shut off all other operating circuits so the ship couldn't be found by their radiation. He equipped himself for travel, and he and Murgatroyd left the Ship. Obviously, he headed toward the city where whatever was wrong was centered.

Travel on foot was unaccustomed, but not difficult. The vegetation was semi-familiar. Maris III was an Earth-type planet and circled a Sol-type sun, and given similar conditions of gravity, air, sunlight, and temperature range, similar organisms should develop. There would be room, for example, for low-growing ground-cover plants, and there would also be advantages to height. There would be some equivalent of grass, and there would be the equivalent of trees, with intermediate forms having in-between habits of growth. Similar reasoning would apply to animal life. There would be parallel ecological niches for animals to fill, and animals would adapt to fill them.

Maris III was not, then, an "unearthly" environment. It was much more like an unfamiliar part of a known planet than a new world altogether. But there were some oddities. An herbivorous creature without legs which squirmed like a snake. A pigeon-sized creature whose wings were modified, gossamer-thin scales with iridescent colorings. There were creatures which seemed to live in lunatic association, and Calhoun was irritably curious to know if they were really symbiotes or only unrecognizable forms of the same organism, like the terrestrial male and female firefly-glowworm.

But he was heading for the city. He couldn't spare time to biologize. On his first day's journey he looked for food to save the rations he carried. Murgatroyd was handy here. The little *tormal* had his place in human society. He was friendly, and he was passionately imitative of human beings, and he had a definite psychology of his own. But he was useful, too. When Calhoun strode through the forests, which had such curiously unleaf-like foliage, Murgatroyd strode grandly with him, imitating his walk. From time to time he dropped to all four paws to investigate something. He invariably caught up with Calhoun within seconds.

Once Calhoun saw him interestedly bite a tiny bit out of a most unpromising-looking shrub stalk. He savored its flavor, and then swallowed it. Calhoun took note of the plant and cut off a section. He bound it to the skin of his arm up near the elbow. Hours later there was no allergic reaction, so he tasted it. It was almost familiar. It had the flavor of a bracken shoot, mingled with a fruity taste. It would be a green bulk-food like spinach or asparagus, filling but without much substance.

Later, Murgatroyd carefully examined a luscious seeming fruit which grew low enough for him to pluck. He sniffed it closely and drew back. Calhoun noted that plant, too. Murgatroyd's tribe was bred at headquarters for some highly valuable qualities. One was a very sensitive stomach—but it was only one. Murgatroyd's metabolism was very close to man's. If he ate something and it didn't disagree with him, it was very likely safe for a man to eat it too. If he rejected something, it probably wasn't. But his real value was much more important than the tasting of questionable foods.

When Calhoun camped the first night, he made a fire of a plant shaped like a cactus barrel and permeated with oil. By heaping dirt around it, he confined its burning to a round space very much like the direct-heat element of an electronic stove. It was an odd illustration of the fact that human progress does not involve anything really new in kind, but only increased convenience and availability of highly primitive comforts. By the light of that circular bonfire. Calhoun actually read a little. But the light was inadequate. Presently he yawned. One did not get very far in the Med Service without knowing probability in human conduct. It enabled one to check on the accuracy of statements made, whether by patients or officials, to a Med Ship man. Today, though, he'd traveled a long way on foot. He glanced at Murgatroyd, who was gravely pretending to read from a singularly straight-edged leaf.

"Murgatroyd," said Calhoun, "it is likely that you will interpret any strange sound as a possible undesirable subjective experience. Which is to say, as dangerous. So if you hear anything sizable coming close during the night, I hope you'll squeal. Thank you."

Murgatroyd said, *"Chee,"* and Calhoun rolled over and went to sleep.

It was mid-morning of the next day when he came upon a cultivated field. It had been cleared and planted, of course, in preparation for the colonists who'd been expected to occupy the city. Familiar Earth plants grew in it, ten feet high and more. And Calhoun examined it carefully, in the hope of finding how long since it had received attention. In his examination, he found the dead man.

As a corpse, the man was brand new, and Calhoun very carefully put himself into a strictly medical frame of mind before he bent over for a technical estimate of what had happened, and when. The dead man seemed to have died of hunger. He was terribly emaciated, and he didn't belong in a cultivated field far from the city. By his garments he was a city dweller and a prosperous one. He wore the jewels that nowadays indicated a man's profession and status in it much more than the value of his possessions. There was money in his pockets, and writing materials, a wallet with pictures and identification, and the normal oddments a man would carry. He'd been a civil servant of the city. And he shouldn't have died of starvation.

He especially shouldn't have gone hungry here! The sweet maize plants were tall and green. Their ears were ripe. He hadn't gone hungry! There were the inedible remains of at least two dozen sweet maize ears. They had been eaten some time— some days—ago, and one had been left unfinished. If the dead man had eaten them but was unable to digest them, his belly should have been swollen with undigested food. It wasn't. He'd eaten and digested and still had died, at least largely of inanition.

Calhoun scowled.

"How about this corn, Murgatroyd?" he demanded.

He reached up and broke off a half-yard-long ear. He stripped away the protecting, stringy leaves. The soft grains underneath looked appetizing. They smelled like good fresh food. Calhoun offered the ear to Murgatroyd.

The little *tormal* took it in his paws and on the instant was eating it with gusto.

"If you keep it down, he didn't die of eating it," said Calhoun, frowning. "And if he ate it—which he did—he didn't die of starvation. Which he did."

He waited. Murgatroyd consumed every grain upon the oversized cob. His furry belly distended a little. Calhoun offered him a second ear. He set to work on that, too, with self-evident enjoyment.

"In all history," said Calhoun, "nobody's ever been able to poison one of you *tormals* because of your digestive system has a qualitative analysis unit in it that yells bloody murder if anything's likely to disagree with you. As a probability of *tormal* reaction, you'd have been nauseated before now if that stuff wasn't good to eat."

But Murgatroyd ate until he was distinctly pot-bellied. He left a few grains on the second ear with obvious regret. He put it down carefully on the ground. He shifted his left-hand whiskers with his paw and elaborately licked them clean. He did the same to the whiskers on the right hand side of his mouth. He said comfortably:

"Chee!"

"Then that's that," Calhoun told him. "This man didn't die of starvation. I'm getting queasy!"

He had his lab kit in his shoulder pack, of course. It was an absurdly small outfit, with almost microscopic instruments. But in Med Ship field work the techniques of microanalysis were standard. Distastefully, Calhoun took the tiny tissue sample from which he could gather necessary information. Standing, he ran through the analytic process that seemed called for. When he finished, he buried the dead man as well as he could and started off in the direction of the city again. He scowled as he walked.

He journeyed for nearly half an hour before he spoke. Murgatroyd accompanied him on all fours now because of his heavy meal. After a mile and a half, Calhoun stopped and said grimly:

"Let's check you over, Murgatroyd."

He verified the *tormal's* pulse and respiration and temperature. He put a tiny breath sample through the part of the lab kit which read off a basic metabolism rate. The small animal was quite accustomed to the process. He submitted blandly. The result of the check over was that Murgatroyd the *tormal* was perfectly normal.

"But," said Calhoun angrily, "that man died of starvation! There was practically no fat in the tissue sample at all! He arrived where we found him while he was strong enough to eat, and he stayed where there was good food, and he ate it, and he digested it, and he died of starvation: Why?"

Murgatroyd wriggled unhappily, because Calhoun's tone was accusing. He said *"Chee!"* in a subdued tone of voice. He looked pleadingly up at Calhoun.

"I'm not really angry with you," Calhoun told him, "but dammit—"

He packed the lab kit back into his pack, which contained food for the two of them for about a week.

"Come along!" he said bitterly. He started off. Ten minutes later he stopped. "What I said was impossible. But it happened, so it mustn't have been what I said. I must have stated it wrongly. He could eat, because he did. He did eat, because of the cobs left. He did digest it. So why did he die of starvation? Did he stop eating?"

"Chee!" said Murgatroyd with conviction.

Calhoun grunted and marched on once more. The man had not died of a disease, not directly. The tissue analysis gave a picture of death which denied that it came of any organ ceasing to function. Was it the failure of the organism—the man—to take the action required for living? Had he stopped eating?

Calhoun's mind skirted the notion warily. It was not plausible. The man had been able to feed himself and had done so. Anything which came upon him and made him unable to feed himself...

"He was a city man," growled Calhoun, "and this is a damned long way from the city. What was he doing out here, anyhow?"

He hesitated and tramped on again. A city man found starved in a remote place might have become lost, somehow or other. But if this man was lost, he was assuredly not without food.

"He belonged in the city," said Calhoun vexedly, "and he left it. The city's almost but not quite empty. Our would-be murderers are in it. This is a new colony. There was a city to be built and fields to be plowed and planted, and then a population was to come here from Dettra Two. The city's built and the fields are plowed and planted. Where's the population?"

He scowled thoughtfully at the ground before him. Murgatroyd tried to scowl too, but he wasn't very successful.

"What's the answer, Murgatroyd? Did the man come away from the city because he had a disease? Was he driven out?"

"Chee," said Murgatroyd without conviction.

"I don't know either," admitted Calhoun. "He walked out into the middle of that field and then stopped walking. He was hungry and he ate. He digested. He stayed there for days. Why? Was he waiting to die of something? Presently he stopped eating. He died. What made him leave the city? What made him stop eating? Why did he die?"

Murgatroyd investigated a small plant and decided that it was not interesting. He came back to Calhoun.

"He wasn't killed," said Calhoun, "but somebody tried to kill us—somebody who's in the city now. That man could have come out here to keep from being killed by the same people. Yet he died anyhow. Why'd they want to kill him? Why'd they want to kill us? Because we were a Med Ship? Because they didn't want Med Service to know there was a disease here? Ridiculous!"

"Chee," said Murgatroyd.

"I don't like the looks of things," said Calhoun. "For instance, in any ecological system there are always carrion eaters. At least some of them fly. There would be plain signs if the city was full of corpses. There aren't any. On the other hand, if the city was inhabited, and there was sickness, they would welcome a Med Ship with open arms. But that dead man didn't come away from the city in any ordinary course of events, and he didn't die in any conventional fashion. There's an empty city and an improbable dead man and a still more improbable attempt at murder! What gives, Murgatroyd?"

Murgatroyd took hold of Calhoun's hand and tugged at it. He was bored. Calhoun moved on slowly.

"Paradoxes don't turn up in nature," said Calhoun darkly. "Things that happen naturally never contradict each other. You only get such things when men try to do things that don't fit together—like having a plague and trying to destroy a Med Ship, if that's the case, and living in a city and not showing on its streets, if that is occurring, and dying of starvation while one's digestion is good and there's food within hand's reach. And that did happen! There was dirty work at the spaceport, Murgatroyd. I suspect dirty work at every crossroad. Keep your eyes open."

"Chee," said Murgatroyd. Calhoun was fully in motion, now, and Murgatroyd let go of his hand and went on ahead to look things over.

Calhoun crossed the top of a rounded hillcrest some three miles from the shallow grave he'd made. He began to accept the idea that the dead man had stopped eating for some reason, as the only possible explanation of his death. But that didn't make it plausible. He saw another ridge of hills ahead.

In another hour he came to the crest of that farther range. It was the worn down remnant of a very ancient mountain chain, now eroded to a mere fifteen hundred or two thousand feet. He stopped at the very top. Here was a time and place to look and take note of what he saw. The ground stretched away in gently rolling fashion for very many miles, and there was the blue blink of sea at the horizon. A little to the left he saw shining white. He grunted.

That was the city of Maris III, which had been built to receive colonists from Dettra and relieve the population pressure there. It had been planned as the nucleus of a splendid, spacious, civilized world-nation to be added to the number of human-occupied worlds. From its beginning it should have held a population in the hundreds of thousands. It was surrounded by cultivated fields, and the air above it should have been a-shimmer with flying things belonging to its inhabitants.

Calhoun stared at it through his binoculars. They could not make an image, even so near, to compare with that which the electron telescope had made from space, but he could see much. The city was perfect. It was intact. It was new. But there was no sign of occupancy anywhere. It did not look dead, so much as frozen. There were no fliers above it. There was no motion on the highways. He saw one straight road which ran directly away along his line of sight. Had there been vehicles on it, he would have seen at least shifting patches of color as clots of traffic moved together. There were none.

He pressed his lips together and began to inspect the nearer terrain. He saw foreshortened areas where square miles of ground had been cleared and planted with Earth vegetation. This was a complicated process. First the ground had to be bulldozed clean, and then great sterilizers had to lumber back and forth, killing every native seed and root and even the native soil bacteria. Then the land had to be sprayed with cultures of the nitrogen-fixing and phosphorous-releasing microscopic organisms which normally live in symbiosis with Earth plants. These had to be tested beforehand for their ability to compete with indigenous bacterial life. And then Earth plants could be sown.

They had been. Calhoun saw that inimitable green which a man somehow always recognizes. It is the green of plants whose ancestors throve on Earth and which have followed that old planet's children halfway across the galaxy.

"There's a look to a well-tended field," said Calhoun, after a long look through binoculars, "that shows what kind of people cultivated it. There are fields up ahead that are well laid out, but nobody's touched them for weeks. The furrows are straight and the crops healthy. But they're beginning to show neglect. If the city was finished and waiting for its population, there would be caretakers tending the fields until the people came. There's been no caretaking done here!"

Murgatroyd stared wisely about as he considered Calhoun to be doing.

"In short," said Calhoun, "something's happened that I don't like. The population must be nearly zero or the fields would have been kept right. One man can keep a hell of a lot of ground in good shape, with modern machinery. People don't plant fields with the intention to neglect them. There's been a considerable change of plans around here. Enmity to a Med Ship is something more than a random impulse." Calhoun was not pleased. With the vision screens of his ship burned out, a return to headquarters was out of the question. "Whoever was handling the landing grid doesn't want help. He doesn't even want visitors. But Med Service was notified to come and look over the new colony. Either somebody changed his views drastically, or the people in charge of the landing grid aren't the ones who asked for a public health checkup."

Murgatroyd said profoundly:

"Chee!"

"The poor devil I buried even seems to hint at something of the sort. He could have used help! Maybe there are two kinds of people here. One kind doesn't want aid and tried to kill us because we'd offer it. The other kind needs it. If so, there might be a certain antagonism…"

He stared with knitted brows over the vast expanse toward the horizon. Murgatroyd, at this moment, was a little way behind Calhoun. He stood up on his hind legs and stared intently off to one side. He shaded his eyes with a forepaw in a singularly humanlike fashion and looked inquisitively at something he saw. Calhoun did not notice.

"Make a guess, Murgatroyd," he commanded. "Make a wild one. A dead man who'd no reason for dying. Live people who should have no reason for wanting to spatter us against the walls of our Med Ship. Something was fatal to that dead man. Somebody tried to be fatal to us. Is there a connection?"

Murgatroyd stared absorbedly at a patch of brushwood some fifty yards to his left. Calhoun started down the hillside. Murgatroyd remained fixed in a pose of intensely curious attention to the patch of brush. Calhoun went on. His back was toward the brush thicket.

There was a deep-toned, musical twanging sound from the thicket. Calhoun's body jerked violently from an impact. He stumbled and went down, with the shaft of a wooden projectile sticking out of his back. He lay still.

Murgatroyd whimpered. He rushed to where Calhoun lay upon the ground. He danced in agitation, chattering shrilly. He wrung his paws in humanlike distress. He tugged at Calhoun, but Calhoun made no response.

A girl emerged from the thicket. She was gaunt and thin, yet her garments had once been of admirable quality. She carried a strange and utterly primitive weapon. She moved toward Calhoun, bent over him and laid a hand to the wooden projectile she had fired into his back.

He moved suddenly. He grappled. The girl toppled, and he swarmed upon her savagely as she struggled. But she was taken by surprise. There was the sound of panting, and Murgatroyd danced in a fever of anxiety.

Then Calhoun stood up quickly. He stared down at the emaciated girl who had tried to murder him from ambush. She was panting horribly now.

"Really," said Calhoun in a professional tone, "as a doctor I'd say that you should be in bed instead of wandering around trying to murder total strangers. When did this trouble begin? I'm going to take your temperature and your pulse. Murgatroyd and I have been hoping to find someone like you. The only other human being I've met on this planet wasn't able to talk."

He swung his shoulder pack around and impatiently jerked a sharp-pointed stick out of it. It was the missile, which had been stopped by the pack. He brought out his lab kit. With absolute absorption in the task, he prepared to make a swift check of his would-be murderer's state of health.

It was not good. There was already marked emaciation. The desperately panting girl's eyes were deep-sunk, hollow. She gasped and gasped. Still gasping, she lapsed into unconsciousness.

"Here," said Calhoun curtly, "you enter the picture, Murgatroyd. This is the sort of thing you're designed to handle."

He set to work briskly. Presently he observed:

"Besides a delicate digestion and a hair-trigger antibody system, Murgatroyd, you ought to have the instincts of a watchdog. I don't like coming that close to being shot by a lady patient. See if there's anybody else around, will you?"

"*Chee,*" said Murgatroyd shrilly. But he didn't understand.

He watched as Calhoun deftly drew a small sample of blood from the unconscious girl's arm and painstakingly put half the tiny quantity into an almost microscopic ampoule in the Lab kit. Then he moved toward Murgatroyd.

The *tormal* wriggled as Calhoun made the injection. But it did not hurt. There was an insensitive spot on his flank where the nerves had been blocked off before he was a week old.

"As one medical man to another," said Calhoun, "you've noticed that the symptoms are of anoxia-oxygen starvation. Which doesn't make sense in the open air where we're breathing comfortably. Another paradox, Murgatroyd! But there's an emergency, too. How can you relieve anoxia when you haven't any oxygen?"

He looked down at the unconscious girl. She displayed the same sort of emaciation he'd noted in the dead man in the field some miles back. Patients with a given disease often acquire a certain odd resemblance to each other. This girl seemed to be in an earlier stage of whatever had killed the civil servant in the corn field. He'd died of starvation with partly eaten food by his hand. She'd tried to murder Calhoun, just as persons unknown, in the city, had tried to kill both Calhoun and Murgatroyd in the Med Ship some forty thousand miles out in space. But her equipment for murder was not on a par with that of the operators of the landing grid. She didn't belong in their class. She might be a fugitive from them.

Calhoun put these things together. Then he swore in sudden, bitter anger. He stopped abruptly, in concern lest she'd heard.

She hadn't. She was still insensible.

CHAPTER THREE

"That pattern of human conduct which is loosely called 'self-respecting' has the curious property of restricting to the individual, through his withdrawal of acts to communicate misfortune, the unfavorable chance occurrences which probability insists must take place. On the other hand, the same pattern of human conduct tends to disseminate and to share chance favorable occurrences among the group. The members of a group of persons practicing 'self-respect,' then, increase the mathematical probability of good fortune to all their number. This explains the instability of cultures in which principles leading to this type of behavior become obsolete. A decadent society brings bad luck upon itself by the operation of the laws of probability..."

Probability and Human Conduct—Fitzgerald

SHE CAME very slowly back to consciousness. It was almost as if she waked from utterly exhausted sleep. When she first opened her eyes, they wandered vaguely until they fell upon Calhoun. Then a bitter and contemptuous hatred filled them. Her hand fumbled weakly to the knife at her waist. It was not a good weapon. It had been table cutlery, and the handle was much too slender to permit a grip by which somebody could be killed. Calhoun bent over and took the knife away from her. It had been ground unskillfully to a point.

"In my capacity as your doctor," he told her, "I must forbid you to stab me. It wouldn't be good for you." Then he said, "Look, my name's Calhoun. I came from Sector Med Headquarters to make a planetary health inspection here, and some lads in the city apparently didn't want a Med Ship aground. So they tried to kill me by buttering me all over the walls of my ship with the landing-grid field. I made what was practically a crash landing, and now I need to know what's up."

The burning hatred remained in her eyes, but there was a trace of doubt.

"Here," said Calhoun, "is my identification."

He showed her the highly official documents which gave him vast authority—where a planetary government was willing to concede it.

"Of course," he added, "papers can be stolen. But I have a witness that I'm what and who I say I am. You've heard of *tormals*? Murgatroyd will vouch for me."

He called his small and furry companion. Murgatroyd advanced and politely offered a small, prehensile paw. He said *"Chee"* in his shrill voice, and then solemnly took hold of the girl's wrist in imitation of Calhoun's previous action of feeling her pulse.

Calhoun watched. The girl stared at Murgatroyd. But all the galaxy had heard of *tormals*. They'd been found on a planet in the Deneb region, and they were engaging pets and displayed an extraordinary immunity to the diseases men were apt to scatter in their interstellar journeying. A forgotten Med Service researcher made an investigation of the ability of *tormals* to live in contact with men. He came up with a discovery which made them very much too valuable to have their lives wasted in mere sociability. There were still not enough of Murgatroyd's kind to meet the need that men had of them, and laymen had to forego their distinctly charming society. So Murgatroyd was an identification.

The girl said faintly:

"If you'd only come earlier...but it's too late now. I—I thought you came from the city."

"I was headed there," said Calhoun.

"They'll kill you."

"Yes," agreed Calhoun, "they probably will. But right now you're ill and I'm Med Service. I suspect there's been an epidemic of some disease here, and that for some reason the people in the city don't want the Med Service to know about it. You seem to have it, whatever it is. Also, that was a very curious weapon you shot me with."

The girl said drearily:

"One of our group had made a hobby of such things. Ancient weapons. He had bows and arrows and—what I shot you with was a crossbow. It doesn't need power. Not even chemical explosives. So when we ran away from the city, he ventured back in and armed us as well as he could."

Calhoun nodded. A little irrelevant talk is always useful at the beginning of a patient-interviewer. But what she said was not irrelevant. A group of people had fled the city. They'd needed arms, and one of their number had gone back into the city for them. He'd known where to find reconstructions of ancient lethal devices—a hobby collection. It sounded like people of the civil service type. Of course there were no longer social classes separated by income. Not on most worlds, anyhow. But there were social groupings based on similar tastes, which had led to similar occupations and went on to natural congeniality. Calhoun placed her now. He remembered a long-outmoded term, "upper middle class," which no longer meant anything in economics but did in medicine.

"I'd like a case history," he said conversationally. "Name?"

"Helen Jons," she said wearily.

He held the mike of his pocket recorder to pick up her answers. Occupation: statistician. She'd been a member of the office force which was needed during the building of the city. When the construction work was finished, most of the workmen returned to the mother-world Dettra, but the office staff stayed on to organize things when the colonists arrived.

"Hold it," said Calhoun. "You were a member of the office staff who stayed in the city to wait for the colonists. But a moment ago you said you fled from the city. There are still some people there, at least around the landing grid. I've reason to be sure of it. Were they part of the office staff too? If not, where did they come from?"

She shook her head weakly.

"Who are they?" he repeated.

"I don't know," she said drearily. "They came after the plague."

"Oh," said Calhoun. "Go on. When did the plague turn up? And how?"

She continued in a feeble voice. The plague appeared among the last shipload of workmen waiting to be returned to the mother world. There were then about a thousand people in the city, of all classes and occupations. The disease appeared first among those who tended the vast fields of planted crops.

It was well established before its existence was suspected. There were no obvious early symptoms, but those affected felt a loss of energy and they became listless and lackadaisical. The listlessness showed first in a cessation of griping and quarreling among the workmen. Normal, healthy human beings are aggressive. They squabble with each other as a matter of course. But squabbling ceased. Men hadn't the energy for it.

Shortness of breath appeared later. It wasn't obvious, at first. Men who lacked energy to squabble wouldn't exert themselves and so get out of breath. It was one of the medical staff who drove himself impatiently in spite of what he thought was a transient weariness, and discovered himself gasping without cause. He took a metabolism test, suspicious because the symptoms were so extreme. His metabolic rate was astonishingly low.

"Hold it again," commanded Calhoun. "You're a statistician, but you're talking medical talk. How's that?"

"Kim," said the girl tiredly. "He was on the medical staff. I was—I was going to marry him."

Calhoun nodded.

"Go on."

She seemed to need to gather strength even to talk. She did not go on. Shortness of breath among the plague victims was progressive. Presently they gasped horribly from the exertion of getting to their feet, even. Walking, however slowly, could be done only at the cost of panting for breath. After a certain time they simply lay still. They could not summon the energy to stir. Then they sank into unconsciousness and died.

"What did the doctors think about all this?" demanded Calhoun.

"Kim could tell you," said the girl exhaustedly. "The doctors worked frantically. They tried everything—everything! They could get the symptoms in experimental animals, but they couldn't isolate the germ or whatever it was that caused the disease. Kim said they couldn't get a pure culture. It was incredible. No technique would isolate the cause of the symptoms, and yet the plague was contagious. Terribly so!"

Calhoun scowled. A new pathogenic mechanism was always possible, but it was at least unlikely. Still, something that standard bacteriological methods couldn't track down was definitely a job for the Med Service. But there were people in the city who didn't want the Med Service to interfere. The girl hadn't referred to them once, when she spoke of a flight from the city, and again when she said someone ventured back for weapons. And she'd used a weapon on him, thinking him from the city. The description of the plague, too, was remarkable.

It was able to hide from men, which was something no other microorganism could accomplish. It was an ability that would offer no advantage to a disease germ in a state of purely natural happenings. Disease germs do not encounter bacteriological laboratories, as a rule, often enough to need to adapt to escape them. It would not help an average germ or microbe to be invisible to an electron microscope. There would be no reason for such invisibility to be developed.

But more than that, why should anybody want to keep a Med Service man like Calhoun from investigating a plague? When infected people fled from the city to die in the wilds, why should people remaining in the city try to destroy a Med Ship which might help to end the deaths? Ordinarily, well people in the middle of an epidemic are terrified lest they catch it. They'd be as anxious for Med Service help as those already infected. What was going on here?

"You said about a thousand people were in the city," observed Calhoun. "They tended the crops and waited for the city's permanent inhabitants. What happened after the plague was recognized to be one?"

"The first shipload of emigrants came from Dettra Two," said the girl hopelessly. "We didn't bring them to ground with the landing grid. Instead, we described the plague. We warned them away. We quarantined ourselves while our doctors tried to fight the disease. The shipload of new people went back to Dettra without landing."

Calhoun nodded. This would be normal.

"Then another ship came. There were maybe two hundred of us left alive. More than half of us already showed signs of the plague. This other ship came. It landed on emergency rockets because we had nobody left who knew how to work the grid."

Then her voice wavered a little as she told of the landing of the strange ship in the landing grid of the city that was dying without ever having really lived. There was no crowd to meet the ship. Those people who were not yet stricken had abandoned the city and scattered themselves widely, hoping to escape contagion by isolating themselves in new and uncontaminated dwelling units. But there was no lack of communication facilities. Nearly all the survivors watched the ship come down through vision screens in the control building of the then-useless grid.

The ship touched ground. Men came out. They did not look like doctors. They did not act like them. The vision screens, in the control building were snapped off immediately. Contact could not be restored. So the isolated groups spoke agitatedly to each other by vision screen. They exchanged messages of desperate hope. Then, newly landed men appeared at an apartment whose occupant was in the act of such a conversation with a group in a distant building. He left the visiphone on as he went to admit and greet the men he hoped were researchers, at least, come to find the cause of the plague and end it.

The viewers at the other visiphone plate gazed eagerly into his apartment. They saw the group of newcomers enter. They saw them deliberately murder their friend and the survivors of his family.

Plague-stricken or merely terrified people—in pairs or trios widely separated through the City—communicated in swift desperation. It was possible that there had been a mistake, a blunder, and an unauthorized crime had been committed. But it was not a mistake. Unthinkable as such an idea was, there developed proof that the plague on Maris III was to be ended as if it were an epizootic among animals. Those who had it and those who had been exposed to it were to be killed to prevent its spread among the newcomers.

A conviction of such horror could not be accepted without absolute proof. But when night fell, the public power supply of the city was cut off and communications ended. The singular sunset hush of Maris III left utter stillness everywhere—except for the screams which echoed among the city's innumerable empty-eyed, unoccupied buildings.

The scant remainder of the plague survivors fled in the night. They fled singly and in groups, carrying the plague with them. Some carried members of their families who were too weak to walk. Others helped already-doomed wives or friends or husbands to the open country. Flight would not save their lives. It would only prevent their murder. But somehow that seemed a thing to be attempted.

"This," said Calhoun, "is not a history of your own case? When did you develop the disease, whatever it may be?"

"Don't you know what it is?" asked Helen hopelessly.

"Not yet," admitted Calhoun. "I've very little information. I'm trying to get more."

He did not mention the information gathered from a dead man in a corn field some miles away.

The girl told of her own case. The first symptom was listlessness. She could pull out of it by making an effort, but it progressed. Day by day more urgent, more violent effort was needed to pay attention to anything, and she noted greater weakness when she tried to act. She felt no discomfort, not even hunger or thirst. She'd had to summon increasing resolution even to become aware of the need to do anything at all.

The symptoms were singularly like those of a man too long at too high an altitude without oxygen. They were even more like those of a man in a non-pressurized flier, whose oxygen supply was cut off. Such a man would pass out without realizing that he was slipping into unconsciousness, only it would happen in minutes. Here the process was infinitely gradual. It was a matter of weeks. But it was the same thing.

"I'd been infected before we ran away," said Helen drearily. "I didn't know it then. Now I know I've a few more days of being able to think and act, if I try hard enough. But it'll be less and less each day. Then I'll stop being able to try."

Calhoun watched the tiny recorder roll its multiple-channel tape from one spool to the other as she talked.

"You had energy enough to try to kill me," he observed.

He looked at the weapon. There was an arched steel spring placed crosswise at the end of a barrel like a sporting blast-gun. Now he saw a handle and a ratchet by which the spring was brought to tension, storing up power to throw the missile. He asked:

"Who wound up this crossbow?"

Helen hesitated. "Kim—Kim Walpole," she said finally.

"You're not a solitary refugee now? There are others of your group still alive?"

She hesitated again, and then said:

"Some of us came to realize that staying apart didn't matter. We couldn't hope to live anyhow. We already had the plague. Kim is one of us. He's the strongest. He wound up the crossbow for me. He had the weapons to begin with."

Calhoun asked seemingly casual questions. She told him of a group of fugitives remaining together because all were already doomed. There had been eleven of them. Two were dead now. Three others were in the last lethargy. It was impossible to feed them. They were dying. The strongest was Kim Walpole, who'd ventured back into the city to bring out weapons for the rest. He'd led them, and now was still the strongest and—so the girl considered—the wisest of them.

They were waiting to die. But the newcomers to the planet—the invaders, they believed—were not content to let them wait. Groups of hunters came out of the city and searched for them.

"Probably," said the girl dispassionately, "to burn our bodies against contagion. They kill us so they won't have to wait. And it just seemed so horrible that we felt we ought to defend our right to die naturally. That's why I shot at you. I shouldn't have, but…"

She stopped helplessly. Calhoun nodded.

The fugitives now aided each other simply to avoid murder. They gathered together exhaustedly at nightfall, and those who were strongest did what they could for the others. By day, those who could walk scattered to separate hiding places, so that if one was discovered, the others might still escape the indignity of being butchered. They had no stronger motive than that. They were merely trying to die with dignity, instead of being killed as sick beasts. Which bespoke a tradition and an attitude that Calhoun approved. People like these would know something of the science of probability in human conduct. Only they would call it ethics. But the strangers—the invaders—were of another type. They probably came from another world.

"I don't like this," said Calhoun coldly. "Just a moment."

He went over to Murgatroyd. Murgatroyd seemed to droop a little. Calhoun checked his breathing and listened to his heart. Murgatroyd submitted, saying only *"Chee"* when Calhoun put him down.

"I'm going to help you to your rendezvous," said Calhoun abruptly. "Murgatroyd's got the plague now. I exposed him to it, and he's reacting fast. And I want to see the others of your group before nightfall."

The girl just managed to get to her feet. Even speaking had tired her, but she gamely though wearily moved off at a slant to the hillside's slope. Calhoun picked up the odd weapon and examined it thoughtfully. He wound it up as it was obviously meant to be. He picked up the missile it had fired, and put it in place. He went after the girl, carrying it. Murgatroyd brought up the rear.

Within a quarter of a mile the girl stopped and clung swaying to the trunk of a slender tree. It was plain that she had to rest, and dreaded getting off her feet because of the desperate effort needed to arise.

"I'm going to carry you," said Calhoun firmly. "You tell me the way."

He picked her up bodily and marched on. She was light. She was not a large girl, but she should have weighed more. Calhoun still carried the quaint antique weapon without difficulty.

Murgatroyd followed as Calhoun went up a small incline on the greater hillside and down a very narrow ravine. Through brushwood he pushed until he came to a small open space where shelters had been made for a dozen or so human beings. They were utterly primitive—merely roofs of leafy branches over framework of sticks. But of course they were not intended for permanent use. They were meant only to protect plague-stricken folk while they waited to die.

But there was disaster here. Calhoun saw it before the girl could. There were beds of leaves underneath the shelters. There were three bodies lying upon them. They would be those refugees in the terminal coma which, since the girl had described it, accounted for the dead man Calhoun had found, dead of starvation with food plants all around him. But now Calhoun saw something more. He swung the girl swiftly in his arms so that she would not see. He put her gently down and said:

"Stay still. Don't move. Don't turn."

He went to make sure. A moment later he raged. It was Calhoun's profession to combat death and illness in all its forms, and he took his profession seriously. There are defeats, of course, which a medical man has to accept, though un-willingly. But nobody in the profession, and least of all a Med Ship man, could fail to be roused to fury by the sight of people who should have been his patients, lying utterly still with their throats cut.

He covered them with branches. He went back to Helen.

"This place has been found by somebody from the city," he told her harshly. "The men in coma have been murdered. I advise you not to look. At a guess, whoever did it is now trying to track down the rest of you."

He went grimly over the small open glade, searching the ground for footprints. There was ground-cover at most places, but at the edge of the clearing he found one set of heavy footprints leading away. He put his own foot beside a print and rested his weight on it. His foot made a lesser depression. The other print had been made by a man weighing more than

Calhoun. Therefore it was not one of the party of plague victims.

He found another set of such footprints, entering the glade from another spot.

"One man only," he said icily. "He won't think he has to be on guard, because a city's administrative personnel—such as was left behind for the plague to hit—doesn't usually have weapons among their possessions. And he's confident that all of you are weak enough not to be dangerous to him."

Helen did not turn pale. She was pale before. She stared numbly at Calhoun. He looked grimly at the sky.

"It'll be sunset within the hour," he said savagely. "If it's the intention of the newcomers—the invaders—to burn the bodies of all plague victims, he'll come back here to dispose of these three. He didn't do it before lest the smoke warn the rest of you. But he knows the shelters held more than three people. He'll be back!"

Murgatroyd said *"Chee!"* in a bewildered fashion. He was on all fours, and he regarded his paws as if they did not belong to him. He panted.

Calhoun checked him over. Respiration away up. Heart action like that of the girl Helen. His temperature was not up, but down. Calhoun said remorsefully:

"You and I, Murgatroyd, have a bad time of it in our profession. But mine is the worse. You don't have to play dirty tricks on me, and I've had to, on you!"

Murgatroyd said *"Chee!"* and whimpered. Calhoun laid him gently on a bed of leaves which was not occupied by a murdered man.

"Lie still!" he commanded. "Exercise is bad for you."

He walked away. Murgatroyd whined faintly, but lay still as if exhausted.

"I'm going to move you," Calhoun told the girl, "so you won't be sighted if that man from the city comes back. And I've got to keep out of sight for a while or your friends will mistake me for him. I count on you to vouch for me later. Basically,

I'm making an ambush." Then he explained irritably, "I daren't try to trail him because he might not backtrack to return here."

He lifted the girl and placed her where she could see the glade in its entirety, but would not be visible. He settled down himself a little distance away. He was acutely dissatisfied with the measures he was forced to take. He could not follow the murderer and leave Helen and Murgatroyd unprotected, even though the murderer might find another victim because he was not being trailed. In any case Murgatroyd's life, just now, was more important than the life of any human being on Maris III. On him depended everything.

But Calhoun was not pleased with himself at all.

There was silence except for the normal noises of living wild things. There were fluting sounds, which later Calhoun would be told came from crawling creatures not too much unlike the land turtles of Earth. There were deep-bass hummings, which came from the throats of miniature creatures which might roughly be described as birds. There were chirpings which were the cries of what might be approximately described as wild pigs, except that they weren't. But the sun Maris sank low toward the nearer hillcrests, and behind them, and there came a strange, expectant hush over all the landscape. At sundown on Maris III there is a singular period when the creatures of the day are silent and those of the night are not yet active. Nothing moved. Nothing stirred. Even the improbable foliage was still.

It was into this stillness and this half-light that small and intermittent rustling sounds entered. Presently there was a faint murmur of speech. A tall, gaunt young man came out of the brushwood, supporting a pathetically feeble old man, barely able to walk. Calhoun made a gesture of warning as the girl Helen opened her lips to speak. The slowly moving pair came into the glade, the young man moving exhaustedly, the older man staggering with weakness despite his help. The younger helped the older to sit down. He stood panting.

A woman and a man came together, assisting each other. There was barely light enough from the sun's afterglow to show their faces, emaciated and white.

A fifth feeble figure came tottering out of another opening in the brush. He was dark-bearded and broad, and he had been a powerful man. But now the plague lay heavily upon him.

They greeted each other listlessly. They had not yet discovered those of their number who had been murdered.

The gaunt young man summoned his strength and moved toward the shelter where Calhoun had covered an unseemly sight with branches.

Murgatroyd whimpered.

There came another rustling sound, but this had nothing of feebleness in it. Branches were pushed forthrightly out of the way and a man came striding confidently into the small open space. He was well-fleshed, and his color was excellent. Calhoun automatically judged him to be in superlative good health, slightly overweight, and of that physical type which suffers very few psychosomatic troubles because it lives strictly and enjoyably in the present.

Calhoun stood up. He stepped out into the fading light just as the sturdy stranger grinned at the group of plague stricken semi-skeletons.

"Back, eh?" he said amiably. "Saved me a lot of trouble. I'll make one job of it."

With leisurely confidence he reached to the blaster at his hip.

"Drop it!" snapped Calhoun from behind him. "Drop it!"

The sturdy man whirled. He saw Calhoun with a crossbow raised to cover him. There was light enough to show that it was not a blast-rifle—in fact, that it was no weapon of any kind modern men would ordinarily use. But much more significant to the sturdy man was the fact that Calhoun wore a uniform and was in good health.

He snatched out his blast-pistol with professional alertness. And Calhoun shot him with the crossbow. It happened that he shot him dead.

CHAPTER FOUR

"Statistically, it must be recognized that no human action is without consequences to the man who acts. Again statistically, it must be recognized that the consequences of an action tend with strong probability to follow the general pattern of the action. A violent action, for example, has a strong probability of violent consequences, and since at least some of the consequences of an act must affect the person acting, a man who acts violently exposes himself to the probability that chance consequences which affect him, if unfavorable, will be violently so."

Probability and Human Conduct—Fitzgerald

MURGATROYD had been inoculated with a blood sample from the girl Helen some three hours or less before sunset. But it was one of the more valuable genetic qualities of the *tormal* race that they reacted to bacterial infection as a human being reacts to medication. Medicine on the skin of a human being rarely has any systemic effect. Medication on mucous membrane penetrates better. Ingested medication—medicine that is swallowed—has greater effectiveness still. But substances injected into tissues or the bloodstream have the most of all. A centigram of almost any drug administered by injection will have an effect close to that of a gram taken orally. It acts at once and there is no modification by gastric juices.

Murgatroyd had had half a cubic centimeter of the girl's blood injected into the spot on his flank where he could feel no pain. It contained the unknown cause of the plague on Maris III. Its effect as injected was incomparably greater than the same infective material smeared on his skin or swallowed. In either such case, of course, it would have had no effect at all, because *tormals* were to all intents and purposes immune to ordinary contagions. Just as they had a built in unit in their digestive tract to cause the instant rejection of unwholesome food, their body cells had a built-in ability to produce antibodies immediately if the toxin of a pathogenic organism came into contact with them. So *tormals* were effectively safe against any disease transmitted by ordinary methods of infection. Yet if a culture of pathogenic bacteria, say, were injected into their bloodstream, their whole body set to work to turn out antibodies because their whole body was attacked, and all at once. There was practically no incubation period.

Murgatroyd, who had been given the plague in mid-afternoon, was reacting violently to its toxins by sunset. But two hours after darkness fell he arose and said shrilly, *"Chee-chee-chee!"* He'd been sunk in heavy slumber. When he woke, there was a small fire in the glade, about which the exhausted, emaciated fugitives consulted with Calhoun. Calhoun was saying bitterly:

"The whole thing is wrong! It's self-contradictory, and that means a man, or men, trying to meddle with the way the universe was made to run. Those characters in the city aren't fighting the plague—they're cooperating with it! When I came in a Med Ship, they should have welcomed my help. Instead they tried to kill me so I couldn't perform the function I was made for and trained for! They're going against the way the universe works. From what Helen tells me, they landed with the purpose of helping the plague wipe out everybody else on the planet. They began their butchery immediately. That's why you people ran away."

The weary, weakened people listened almost numbly.

"The invaders—and that's what they are," said Calhoun angrily, "have to be immune and know it, or else they wouldn't risk contagion by tracking you down to murder you. The city's infected and they're not alarmed. You're dying and they only try to hasten your death. I arrive, and I might be of use, so they try to kill me. They must know what the plague is and what it does, because their only criticism of it seems to be that it doesn't kill fast enough. And that is out of the ordinary course of nature. It's not intelligent human conduct.

Murgatroyd peered about. He'd just waked, and the look of his surroundings had changed entirely while he slept.

"A plague's not pleasant, but it's natural. This plague is neither pleasant *nor* natural. There's human interference with the normal course of events—certainly the way things are going is abnormal. I'm not too sure somebody didn't direct this from the beginning. That's why I shot that man with the crossbow instead of taking a blaster to him. I meant to wound him so I could make him answer questions, but the crossbow's not an accurate weapon and it happened that I killed him instead. There wasn't much information in the stuff in his pockets. The only significant item was a ground-car key, and that only means there's a car waiting for him to come back from hunting you."

The gaunt young man said drearily:

"He didn't come from Dettra, which is our planet. Fashions are different on different worlds and he wears a uniform we don't have. His Clothing uses fasteners we don't use, too. He's from another solar system entirely."

Murgatroyd saw Calhoun and rushed to him. He embraced Calhoun's legs with enthusiasm. He chattered shrilly of his relief at finding the man he knew. The skeleton like plague victims stared at him.

"This," said Calhoun with infinite relief, "is Murgatroyd. He's had the plague and is over it. So now we'll get you people cured. I wish I had better light!"

He counted Murgatroyd's breathing and listened to his heart. Murgatroyd was in that state of boisterous good health which is standard in any well-cared-for lower animal, but amounts to genius in a *tormal*. Calhoun regarded him with deep satisfaction.

"All right!" he said. "Come along!"

He plucked a brand of burning resinous stuff from the campfire. He handed it to the gaunt young man and led the way. Murgatroyd ambled complacently after him. Calhoun stopped under one of the unoccupied shelters and got out his lab kit. He bent over Murgatroyd. What he did, did not hurt. When he stood up, he squinted at the red fluid in the instrument he'd used.

"About twenty ccs," he observed. "This is strictly emergency stuff I'm doing now. But I'd say that there's an emergency."

The gaunt young man said:

"I'd say you've doomed yourself. The incubation period seems to be about six days. It took that long to develop among the doctors we had on the office staff."

Calhoun opened a compartment of the kit, whose minuscule test tubes and pipettes gleamed in the torchlight. He absorbedly transferred the reddish fluid to a miniature filter barrel, piercing a self-healing plastic cover to do so. He said:

"You're pre-med of course. The way you talk—"

"I was an interne," said Kim. "Now I'm pre-corpse."

"I doubt that last," said Calhoun. "But I wish I had some distilled water…this is anticoagulant." He added the trace of a drop to the sealed, ruddy fluid. He shook the whole filter to agitate it. The instrument was hardly larger than his thumb. "Now a dumper…" He added a minute quantity of a second substance from an almost microscopic ampule. He shook the filter again. "You can guess what I'm doing. With a decent lab I'd get the structure and formula of the antibody Murgatroyd has so obligingly turned out for us. We'd set to work synthesizing it, and in twenty hours we would have it coming out of the reaction flasks in quantity. But there is no lab."

"There's one in the city," said the gaunt young man hopelessly. "It was for the colonists who were to come. And we were staffed to give them proper medical care. When the plague came, our doctors did everything imaginable. They not only tried the usual culture tricks, but they cultured samples of every separate tissue in fatal cases. They never found a single organism, even with electron microscopes, that would produce the plague." He said with a sort of weary pride, "Those who'd been exposed worked until they had the plague, and then others took over. Every man worked as long as he could make his brain serve him."

Calhoun squinted through the glass tube of the filter at the light of the sputtering torch.

"Almost clumped," he said. Then he added, "I suspect there's been some very fine laboratory work done somewhere to give the invaders their confidence of immunity to this plague. They landed and instantly set to work to mop up the city—to complete the job the plague hadn't quite finished. I suspect there could have been some fine lab work done to make plague mechanism undetectable. I don't like the things I'm forced to suspect!"

He inspected the glass filter tube again.

"Somebody," he said coldly, "considered that my arrival would be an unfavorable circumstance to him and what he wanted to happen. I think it is. He tried to kill me. He didn't. I'm afraid I consider his existence an unfavorable circumstance." He paused, and said very measuredly, "Co-operating with a plague is a highly technical business; it needs as much information as fighting a plague. Cooperation could no more be done from a distance than fighting it. If the invaders had come to fight the plague, they'd have sent their best medical men to help. If they came to assist it, they'd have sent butchers, but they'd also send the very best man they had to make sure that nothing went wrong with the plague itself. The logical man to be field director of the extermination project would be the man who'd worked out the plague himself." He paused again, and said icily, "I'm no judge to pass on anybody's guilt or innocence or fate, but as a Med Service man I've authority to take measures against health hazards!"

He began to press the plunger of the filter, judging by the wavering light of the torch. The piston was itself the filter, and on one side a clear, mobile liquid began very slowly to appear.

"Just to be sure, though—you said there was a lab in the city and the doctors found nothing."

"Nothing," agreed Kim hopelessly. "There'd been a complete bacteriological survey of the planet. Nothing new appeared. Everybody's oral and intestinal flora were normal. Naturally, no alien bug would be able to compete with the strains we humans have been living with for thousands of years. So there wasn't anything unknown in any culture from any patient."

"There could have been a mutation," said Calhoun. He watched the clear serum increase. "But if your doctors couldn't pass the disease—"

"They could!" said Kim bitterly. "A massive shot of assorted bugs would pass it, breathed or swallowed or smeared on the skin. Experimental animals could be given the plague. But no one organism could be traced as giving it. No pure culture would!"

Calhoun continued to watch the clear fluid develop on the delivery side of the filter piston. Presently there was better than twelve cubic centimeters of clear serum on one side, and an almost solid block of clumped blood cells on the other. He drew off the transparent fluid with a fine precision.

"We're working under far from asceptic conditions," he said wryly, "but we have to take the chances. Anyhow, I'm getting a hunch. A pathogenic mechanism that isn't a single, identifiable bug—it's not natural. It smells of the laboratory, just as uniformed murderers who are immune to a plague do. It's not too wild a guess to suspect that somebody worked out the plague as well as the immunization of the invaders. That it was especially designed to baffle the doctors who might try to fight it."

"It did," agreed Kim bitterly.

"So," said Calhoun, "maybe a pure culture wouldn't carry the plague. Maybe the disaster-producing apparatus simply isn't there when you make pure cultures. There's even a reason to suspect something specific. Murgatroyd was a very sick animal. I've only known of one previous case in which a *tormal* reacted as violently as Murgatroyd did to an injection. That case had us sweating!"

"If I were going to live," said Kim grimly, "I might ask what it was."

"Since you're going to," Calhoun told him, "I'll tell you. It was a pair of organisms. Separately, they were so near harmless as makes no difference. Together, their toxins combined to be pure poison. It was synergy. They were a synergic pair, which, together, were like high explosive. That one was the devil to track down!"

He went back across the glade. Murgatroyd came skipping after him, scratching at the anesthetic patch on his side.

"You go first," said Calhoun briefly to Helen Jons. "This is an antibody serum. You may itch afterward, but I doubt it. Your arm, please."

She bared her pitifully thin arm. He gave her practically a cc of fluid which—plus blood corpuscles and some forty-odd other essential substances—had been circulating in Murgatroyd's bloodstream not long since. The blood corpuscles had been clumped and removed by one compound plus the filter, and the anticoagulant had neatly modified most of the others. In a matter of minutes, the lab kit had prepared as usable a serum as any animal-using technique would produce. Logically, the antibodies it contained should be isolated and their chemical structure determined. They should be synthesized, and the synthetic antibody-complex administered to plague victims. But Calhoun faced a group of people doomed to die. He could only use his field kit to produce a small-scale miracle for them. He could not do a mass-production job.

"Next!" said Calhoun. "Tell them what it's all about, Kim."

The gaunt young man bared his own arm. "If what he says is so, this will cure us. If isn't so, nothing can do us any more harm."

And Calhoun briskly gave them, one after another, the shots of what ought to be a curative serum for an unidentified disease which he suspected was not caused by any single germ, but by a partnership. Synergy is an acting together. Charcoal will burn quietly. Liquid air will not burn at all. But the two together constitute a violent explosive. The ancient simple drug sulfa is not intoxicating. A glass of wine is not intoxicating. But the two together have the kick of dynamite. Synergy in medicine is a process by which, when one substance with one effect is given in combination with another substance with another effect, the two together have the consequences of a third substance intensified to fourth or fifth or tenth power.

"I think," said Calhoun when he'd finished, "that by morning you'll feel better—perhaps cured of the plague entirely and only weak from failure to force yourselves to take nourishment. If it turns out that way, then I advise you all to get as far away from the city as possible for a considerable while. I think this planet is going to be repopulated. I suspect that shiploads of colonists are on the way here now, but not from Dettra, which built the city. And I definitely guess that, sick or well, you're going to be in trouble if or when you contact the new colonists."

They looked tiredly at him. They were a singular lot of people. Each one seemed half-starved, yet their eyes had not the brightness of suffering. They looked weary beyond belief, and yet there was no self-neglect. They were of that singular human type which maintains human civilization against the inertia of the race, because it drives itself to get needed things done. It is not glamorous, this dogged part of mankind which keeps things going. It is sometimes absurd. For dying folk to wash themselves when even such exertion calls for enormous resolution is not exactly rational. To help each other try to die with dignity was much more a matter of self-respect than of intellectual decision. But as a Med Ship man, Calhoun viewed them with some warmth. They were the type that has to be called on when an emergency occurs and the wealth-gathering type tends to flee and the low-time-sense part of a population inclines to riot or loot or worse.

Now they waited listlessly for their own deaths.

"There's no exact precedent for what's happened here," explained Calhoun. "A thousand years or so ago there was a king of France—a country back on old Earth—who tried to wipe out a disease called leprosy by executing all the people who had it. But lepers were a nuisance. They couldn't work. They had to be fed by charity. They died in inconvenient places and only other lepers dared handle their bodies. They tended to throw normal human life out of kilter. That wasn't the case here. The man I killed wanted you dead for another reason. He and his friends wanted you dead right away."

The gaunt Kim Walpole said tiredly:

"He wanted to dispose of our bodies in a sanitary fashion."

"Nonsense!" snapped Calhoun. "The city's infected. You lived, ate, breathed, walked in it. Nobody can dare use that city unless they know how the contagion's transmitted, and how to counteract it. Your own colonists turned back. These men wouldn't have landed if they hadn't known they were safe!"

There was silence.

"If the plague is an intended crime," added Calhoun, "you are the witnesses to it. You've got to be gotten rid of before colonists from somewhere other than Dettra arrive here."

The dark-bearded man growled:

"Monstrous! Monstrous!"

"Agreed," said Calhoun. "But there's no interstellar government now, any more than there was a planetary government in the old days back on Earth. So if somebody pirates a colony ready to be occupied, there's no authority able to throw them out. The only recourse would be war. And nobody is going to start an interplanetary war—not with the bombs that can be landed! If the invaders can land a population here, they can keep it here. It's piracy, with nobody able to do anything to the pirates." He paused, and said with irony, "Of course they could be persuaded that they were wrong."

But that was not even worth thinking about. In the computation of probabilities in human conduct, self-interest is a high-value factor. Children and barbarians have clear ideas of justice due *to* them, but no idea at all of justice due *from* them. And though human colonies spread toward the galaxy's rim, there was still a large part of every population which was civilized only in that it could use tools. Most people still remained comfortably barbaric or childish in their emotional lives. It was a fact that had to be considered in Calhoun's profession. It bore remarkably on matters of contagion, and health, and life itself.

"You'll have to hide. Perhaps permanently," he told them. "It depends partly on what happens to me, however, I have to go into the city. There's a very serious health problem there.

Kim said with irony:

"In the city? Everybody's healthy there. There're so healthy that they come out to hunt us down for sport!"

"Considering that the city's thoroughly infected, their immunity is a health problem," said Calhoun. "But besides that, it looks like the original cause of the plague is there, too. I'd guess that the originator of this plague is technical director of the exterminating operation that's in progress on this planet. I'd guess he's in the ship that brought the butcher-invaders. I'd be willing to bet that he's got a very fine laboratory on the ship."

Kim stared at him. He clenched and unclenched his hands.

"And I'd say it ought to be quite useless to fight this plague before that man and that laboratory were taken care of," said Calhoun. "You people are probably all right. I think you'll wake up feeling better. You may be well. But if the plague is artificial, if it was developed to make a colony planet useless to the world that built it, but healthy for people who want to seize it..."

"What?"

"It may be the best plague that was developed for the purpose, but you can be sure it's not the only one. Dozens of strains of deadly bugs would have to be developed to be sure of getting the deadliest. Different kinds of concealment would have to be tried, in case somebody guessed the synergy trick, as I did, and could do something about the first plague used.

There'd have to be a second and third and fourth plague available. You see?"

Kim nodded, speechless.

"A setup like that is a real health hazard," said Calhoun. "As a Med Service man, I have to deal with it. It's much more important than your life or mine or Murgatroyd's. So I have to go into the city to do what can be done. Meanwhile, you'd better lie down now. Give Murgatroyd's antibodies a chance to work."

Kim started to move away. Then he said:

"You've been exposed. Have you protected yourself?"
"Give me a quarter-cc shot," said Calhoun. "That should do."

He handed the injector to the gaunt young man. He noted the deftness with which Kim handled it. Then he helped get the survivors of the original group—there were six of them now—to the leafy beds under the shelters. They were very quiet, even more quiet than their illness demanded. They were very polite. The old man and woman who'd struggled back to the glade together made a special effort to bid Calhoun good night with the courtesy appropriate to city folk of tradition.

Calhoun settled down to keep watch through the night. Murgatroyd snuggled confidingly close to him. There was silence.

But not complete silence. The night of Maris III was filled with tiny noises, and some not so faint. There were little squeaks which seemed to come from all directions, including overhead. There were chirpings which were definitely at ground level. There was a sound like effortful grunting in the direction of the hills. In the lowlands there was a rumbling which moved very slowly from one place to another. By its rate of motion, Calhoun guessed that a pack or herd of small animals was making a night journey and uttering deep-bass noises as it traveled.

He debated certain grim possibilities. The man he'd killed had had a ground-car key in his pocket. He'd probably come out in a powered vehicle. He might have had a companion, and the method of hunting down fugitives—successful, in his case—was probably well established. That companion might come looking for him, so watchfulness was necessary.

Meanwhile, there was the plague. The idea of synergy was still most plausible. Suppose the toxins—the poisonous metabolic products—of two separate kinds of bacteria combined to lessen the ability of the blood to carry oxygen and scavenge away carbon dioxide? It would be extremely difficult to identify the pair, and the symptoms would be accounted for. No pure culture of any organism to be found would give the plague. Each, by itself, would be harmless. Only a combination of the two would be injurious. And if so much was assumed, and the blood lost its capacity to carry oxygen, mental listlessness would be the first symptom of all. The brain requires a high oxygen level in its blood supply if it is to work properly. Let a man's brain be gradually, slowly, starved of oxygen and all the noted effects would follow. His other organs would slow down, but at a lesser rate. He would not remember to eat. His blood would still digest food and burn away its own fat—though more and more sluggishly, while his brain worked only foggily. He would become only semiconscious, and then there would come a time of coma when unconsciousness claimed him and his body lived on only as an idling machine, until it ran out of fuel and died.

Calhoun tried urgently to figure out a synergic combination which might make a man's blood cease to do its work. Perhaps only minute quantities of the dual poison might be needed. It might work as an anti-vitamin or an anti-enzyme, or—

The invaders of the city were immune, though. Quite possibly the same antibodies Murgatroyd had produced were responsible for their safety. Somewhere, somebody had very horribly used the science of medicine to commit a monstrous crime. But medicine was still a science. It was still a body of knowledge of natural law. And natural laws are consistent and work together toward that purpose for which the universe was made.

He heard a movement across the clearing. He reached for his blaster. Then he saw what the motion was. It was Kim Walpole, intolerably weary, trudging with infinite effort to where Helen Jons lay. Calhoun heard him ask heavily:

"You're all right?"

"Yes, Kim," said the girl softly. "I couldn't sleep. I'm wondering if we can hope."

Kim did not answer.

"If we live..." said the girl yearningly. She stopped.

Calhoun felt that he ought to put his fingers in his ears. The conversation was strictly private. But he needed to be on guard, so he coughed, to give notice that he heard. Kim called to him:

"Calhoun?"

"Yes," said Calhoun. "If you two talk, you should do it in whispers. I'm going to watch in case the man I killed had a companion who might come looking for him. One question, though. If the plague is artificial, it had to be started. Did a ship land here two weeks or a month before your workmen began to be ill? It could have come from anywhere."

"There was no landing of any ship," said Kim. "No."

Calhoun frowned. His reasoning seemed airtight. The plague must have been introduced here from somewhere else!

"There had to be," he insisted. "Any kind of ship! From anywhere!"

"There wasn't," repeated Kim. "We had no off-planet communication for three months before the plague appeared. There's been no ship here at all except from Dettra, with supplies and workmen and that sort of thing."

Calhoun scowled. This was impossible. Then Helen's voice sounded very faintly. Kim made a murmurous response. Then he said:

"Helen reminds me that there was a queer roll of thunder one night not long before the plague began. She's not sure it means anything, but in the middle of the night, with all the stars shining, thunder rolled back and forth across the sky above the city. This was a week or two before the plague. It waked everybody. Then it rolled away to the horizon and beyond. The weather people had no explanation for it.

Calhoun considered. Murgatroyd nestled still closer to him. He snapped his fingers suddenly.

"That was it!" he said savagely. "That's the trick! I haven't all the answers, but I know some very fine questions to ask now. And I think I know where to ask them."

He settled back. Murgatroyd slept. There was the faintest possible murmur of voices where Kim Walpole and the girl Helen talked wistfully of the possibility of hope.

Calhoun contemplated the problem before him. There were very, very few survivors of the people who belonged in the city. There was a shipload of murderers—butchers!—who had landed to see that the last of them were destroyed. Undoubtedly there was a highly trained and probably brilliant microbiologist in the invaders' expedition. One would be needed, to make sure of the success of the plague and to verify the absolute protection of the butchers, so that other colonists could come here to take over and use the planet. There could be no failure of protection for the people not of Dettra who expected to inhabit this world. There would have to be completely competent supervision of this almost unthinkable, this monstrous stealing of a world.

"The plague would probably be a virus pair," muttered Calhoun. "Probably introduced and scattered by a ship with wings *and* rockets. It'd have wings because it wouldn't want to land, but did want to sweep back and forth over the city. It'd drop frozen pellets of the double virus culture. They'd drop down toward the ground, melting and evaporating as they fell, and they'd flow over the city as an invisible, descending blanket of contagion coating everything. Then the ship would head away over the horizon and out to space on its rockets. Its wings wouldn't matter out of atmosphere, and it'd go into overdrive and go back home to wait...

He felt an icy anger, more savage than any rage could be. With this technique, a confederation of human beings utterly without pity could become parasitic on other worlds. They could take over any world by destroying its people, and no other people could make any effective protest, because the stolen world would be useless except to the murderers who had taken it over. This affair on Maris III might be merely a test of the new ruthlessness. The murderer-planet could spread its ghastly culture like a cancer through the galaxy.

But there were two other things involved beside a practice of conquest through murder by artificial plagues. One was what would happen to the people—the ordinary, commonplace citizens—of a civilization which spread and subsisted by such means. It would not be good for them. In the aggregate, they'd be worse off than the people who died.

The other?

"They might make a field test of their system," said Calhoun very coldly, "without doing anything more serious to the Med Service than killing one man—me—and destroying one small Med Ship. But they couldn't adopt this system on any sort of scale without destroying the Med Service first. I'm beginning to dislike this business excessively!"

CHAPTER FIVE

"Very much of physical science is merely the comprehension of long-observed facts. In human conduct there is a long tradition of observation, but a very brief record of comprehension. For example, human lives in contact with other human lives follow the rules of other ecological systems. All too often, however, a man imagines that an ecological system is composed only of things, whereas such a system operates through the actions of things. It is not possible for any part of an ecological complex to act upon the other parts without being acted upon in its turn. So that it follows that it is singularly stupid—but amazingly common—for an individual to assume human society to be passive and

unreactive. He may assume that he can do what he pleases, but inevitably there is a reaction as energetic as his action, and as well-directed. Moreover, probability..."

Probability and Human Conduct—Fitzgerald

AN HOUR after sunrise Calhoun's shoulder pack was empty of food. The refugees arose, and they were weak and ravenous. Their respiration had slowed to normal. Their pulses no longer pounded. Their eyes were no longer dull, but very bright. But they were in advanced states of malnutrition, and now were aware of it. Their brains were again receiving adequate oxygen and their metabolism was at normal level—and they knew they were starving.

Calhoun served as cook. He trudged to the spring that Helen described. He brought back water. While they sucked on sweet tablets from his rations and watched with hungry eyes, he made soup from the dehydrated rations he'd carried for Murgatroyd and himself. He gave it to them as the first thing their stomachs were likely to digest.

He watched as they fed themselves. The elderly man and woman sipped delicately, looking at each other. The man with the broad dark beard ate with tremendous self-restraint. Helen fed the weakest, oldest man, between spoonfuls for herself, and Kim Walpole ate slowly, brooding.

Calhoun kept them going, slowly providing them with food, until he had no more to offer. By then they had made highly satisfying gains in strength. But it was then late morning.

He drew Kim aside.

"During the night," he said, "I got another lot of serum ready. I'm leaving it with you, with an injector. You'll find other fugitives. I gave you massive doses. You'd better be stingy. Try half-cc shots. Maybe you can skimp that."

"What about you?" demanded Kim.

Calhoun shrugged.

"I've got an awful lot of authority, if I can make it stick," he said drily. "As a Med Ship man I've power to take complete charge of any health emergency. You people have a plague here. That's one emergency. It's artificial. That's another. The people who've spread it here have reason, in their success to date on this planet, to think they can take over any other world they choose. And, human nature being what it is, that's the biggest health hazard in history. I've got to get to work on it."

"There's a shipload of armed murderers here," said Kim.

"I'm not much interested in them," admitted Calhoun. "I want to get at the man who's at the head of this thing. As I told you, he should have other plagues in stock. It's entirely possible that the operation here is no more than a small-scale field test of a new technique for conquest."

"If those butchers find you, you'll be killed."

"True," admitted Calhoun. "But the number of chance happenings that could favor me is much greater than the number that could favor them. I'm working with nature, and they're working against it. Anyhow, as a Med Service man, I should prevent the landing of anybody—anybody at all—on a plague-stricken planet like this. And I suspect that there are plans for landings. I should set up an effective quarantine."

His tone was dry. Kim Walpole stared.

"You mean you'll try to stop them?"

"I shall try," said Calhoun, "to implement the authority vested in me by the Med Service for such cases as this. The rules about quarantine are rather strict."

"You'll be killed," said Kim again.

Calhoun ignored the repeated prediction.

"That invader found you," he observed, "because he knew that you'd have to drink. So he found a brook and followed it up, looking for signs of humans drinking from it. He found footprints about the spring. I found his footprints there, too. That's the trick you'll use to find other fugitives. But pass on the word not to leave tracks hereafter. For other advice, I advise you to get all the weapons you can. Modern ones, of course. You've got the blaster from the man I killed."

"I think," said Kim between his teeth, "that I'll get some more. If hunters from the city do track us to our drinking places, I'll know how to get more weapons!"

"Yes," agreed Calhoun. "Now, Murgatroyd made the anti-bodies that cured you. As a general rule, you can expect antibody production in your own bodies once an infection begins to be licked. In case of extreme emergency, each of you can probably supply antibodies for a fair number of other plague victims. You might try serum from blisters you produce on your skin. Quite often antibodies turn up there. I don't guarantee it, but sometimes it works."

He paused. Kim Walpole said harshly:

"But you! Isn't there anything we can do for you?"

"I was going to ask you something," said Calhoun. He produced the telephoto films of the city as photographed from space. "There's a laboratory in the city. A biochemistry lab. Show me where to look for it."

Walpole gave explicit directions, pointing out the spot on the photo. Calhoun nodded. Then Kim said fiercely:

"But tell us something we can do! We'll be strong, presently, and we'll have weapons. We'll track downstream to where hunters leave their ground-cars and be equipped with them. We can help you!"

Calhoun nodded approvingly.

"Right. If you see the smoke of a good-sized fire in the city, and if you've got a fair number of fairly strong men with you, and if you've got ground-cars, you might investigate. But be cagey about it. Very cagey!"

"If you signal we'll come," said Kim Walpole grimly, "no matter how few we are."

"Fine," said Calhoun. He had no intention of calling on these weakened, starving people for help.

He swung his depleted pack on his back again and slipped away from the glade. He made his way to the spring, which flowed up clear and cool from unseen depths. He headed down the little brook which flowed away from it. Murgatroyd raced along its banks. He hated to get his paws wet. Presently, where the underbrush grew thickly close to the water's edge, Murgatroyd wailed, *"Chee! Chee!"* Calhoun plucked him from the ground and set him on his shoulder. Murgatroyd clung blissfully there as Calhoun followed down the stream-bed. He adored being carried.

Two miles down, there was another cultivated field. This one was planted with an outsized root crop, and Calhoun walked past shoulder-high bushes with four-inch blue-and-white flowers. He recognized the plant as one of the family Solanaceae-belladona was still used in medicine—but he couldn't identify it until he dug up a root and found a tuber. But the six-pound specimen he uncovered was still too young and green to be eaten. Murgatroyd refused to touch it.

Calhoun was ruefully considering the limitations of specialized training when he came to the end of the cultivated field. There was a highway. It was new, of course. City, fields, highways and all the physical aspects of civilized life had been built on this planet before the arrival of the colonists who were to inhabit it. It was extraordinary to see such preparations for a population not yet on hand. But Calhoun was much more interested in the ground-car he found waiting on the highway, hard by a tiny bridge under which a small brook flowed.

The key he'd taken from the dead invader fitted. He got in the car and beckoned Murgatroyd to the seat beside him.

"Characters like the man I killed, Murgatroyd," he observed, "aren't very important. There're mere butchers—killers. That sort of character likes to loot. There's nothing here for them to loot. They're bound to be bored. They're bound to be restless. We won't have much trouble with them. I'm worrying about the man who possibly designed and is certainly supervising the action of the plague. I look for trouble with him."

The ground-car was in motion then, toward the city. He drove on.

It was a good twenty miles, but he did not encounter a single other vehicle. Presently the city lay spread out before him. He surveyed it thoughtfully. It was very beautiful. Fifty generations of architects on many worlds had played with stone and steel, groping for perfection. This city was a close approach. There were towers which glittered whitely, and low buildings which seemed to nestle on the vegetation covered ground. There were soaring bridges and gracefully curving highways, and park areas laid out and ready. There was no monotony anywhere.

The only exception to gracefulness was the massive landing grid, half a mile and a mile across, which was a lacework of monster steel girders with spider-thin wires of copper woven about them in the complex curves its operation required. Inside it, Calhoun could see the ship of the invaders. It had landed in the grid enclosure, and later Calhoun had blown out the transformers of the grid. They were probably in process of repair now. But the ship stood sturdily on the ground inside the great structure that dwarfed it.

"The man we're after will be in that ship, Murgatroyd," said Calhoun. "He'll have inner and outer lock-doors fastened, and he'll be inside a six-inch beryllium-steel wall. Rather difficult to break in upon. And he'll be uneasy. An intellectual type gone wrong doesn't feel at ease with the kind of butchers he has to associate with. I think the problem is to get him to invite us into his parlor. But it may not be simple."

"Chee," said Murgatroyd doubtfully.

"Oh, we'll manage," Calhoun assured him. "Somehow!"

He spread out his photographs. Kim Walpole had marked where he should go and a route to it. Having been in the city while it was being built, he knew even the service lanes which, being sunken, were not a part of the city's good looks.

"But the invaders," explained Calhoun, "won't deign to use grubby service lanes. They consider themselves aristocrats because they were sent to be conquerors, though the work required of them was simple butchery. I wonder what sort of swine run the world they came from!"

He put away the photos and headed for the city again. He branched off the main highway, near the city. A turn-off descended into a cut. The road in the cut was intended for loads of agricultural produce entering the city. It was strictly utilitarian. It ran below the surface of the park areas, and entered the city without pride. When among the buildings it ran between rows of undecorative gates, behind which waste matter was destined to be collected to be carted away as fertilizer for the fields. The city was very well designed.

Rolling through the echoing sunken road, Calhoun saw, just once, a ground-car in motion on a far-flung, cobwebby bridge between two tall towers. It was high overhead. Nobody in it would be watching grubby commerce roads.

The whole affair was very simple indeed. Calhoun brought the car to a stop beneath the overhang of a balconied building many stories high. He got out and opened the gate. He drove the car into the cavernous, so-far-unused lower part of the building. He closed the gate behind him. He was in the center of the city, and his presence was unknown. This was at three or later in the afternoon.

He climbed a clean new flight of steps and came to the sections the public would use. There were glassy walls which changed their look as one moved between them. There were the lifts. Calhoun did not try to use them. He led Murgatroyd up the circular ramps which led upward in case of unthinkable emergency. He and Murgatroyd plodded up and up. Calhoun kept count.

On the fifth level there were signs of use, while all the others had that dusty cleanness of a structure which has been completed but not yet occupied.

"Here we are," said Calhoun cheerfully.

But he had his blaster in his hand when he opened the door of the laboratory. It was empty. He looked approvingly about as he hunted for the storeroom. It was a perfectly equipped biological laboratory, and it had been in use. Here the few doomed physicians awaiting the city's population had worked desperately against the plague. Calhoun saw the trays of cultures they'd made, dried up and dead now. Somebody had turned over a chair. Probably when the laboratory was searched by the invaders, in case someone not of their kind still remained alive in it.

He found the storeroom. Murgatroyd watched with bright eyes as he rummaged.

"Here we have the things men use to cure each other," said Calhoun oracularly. "Practically every one a poison save for its special use! Here's an assortment of spores—pathogenic organisms, Murgatroyd. They have their uses. And here are drugs which are synthesized nowadays, but are descended from the poisons found on the spears of savages. Great helps in medicine. And here are the anesthetics—poisons too. These are what I am counting on."

He chose, very painstakingly. Dextrethyl. Polysulfate. The one marked inflammable and dangerous. The other with the maximum permissible dose on its label, and the names of counteracting substances which would neutralize it. He burdened himself. Murgatroyd reached up a paw. Since Calhoun was carrying something, he wanted to carry something too.

They went down the circular ramp again as sunset drew near. Calhoun searched once more in the below-surface levels of the buildings. He found what he wanted—a painter's vortex-gun that would throw "smoke rings" of tiny paint droplets at a wall or object to be painted. One could vary the size of the ring at impact from a bare inch to a three-foot spread.

Calhoun cleaned the paint-gun. He was meticulous about it. He filled its tank with dextrethyl brought down from the laboratory. He piled the empty containers out of sight.

"This trick," he observed, as he picked up the paint-gun again, "was devised to be used on a poor devil of a lunatic who carried a bomb in his pocket for protection against imaginary assassins. It would have devastated a quarter-mile circle, so he had to be handled gently."

He patted his pockets. He nodded.

"Now we go hunting—with an oversized atomizer loaded with dextrethyl. I've polysulphate and an injector to secure each specimen I knock over. Not too good, eh? But if I have to use a blaster I'll have failed."

He looked out a window at the sky. It was now late dusk. He went back to the gate to the service road. He went out and carefully closed it behind him. On foot, with many references to the photomaps, he began to find his way toward the landing grid. It ought to be something like the center of the invaders' location.

It was dark when he climbed other service stairs from the cellar of another building. This was the communications building of the city. It had been the key to the mopping-up process the invaders began on landing. Its callboard would show which apartments had communicators in use. When such a call showed, a murder party could be sent to take care of the caller. Even after the first night, some individual, isolated folk might remain, unaware of what was happening. So there would be somebody on watch, just in case a dying man called for the solace of a human voice while still he lived.

There was a man on watch. Calhoun saw a lighted room. Paint-gun ready, he moved very silently toward it. Murgatroyd padded faithfully behind him.

Outside the door, Calhoun adjusted his curious weapon. He entered. The man nodded in a chair before the lifeless board. When Calhoun entered he raised his head and yawned. He turned.

Calhoun sprayed him with smoke rings—vortex rings. But the rings were spinning missiles of vaporized dextrethyl, that anesthetic developed from ethyl chloride some two hundred years before, and not yet bettered for its special uses. One of its properties was that the faintest whiff of its vapor produced a reflex impulse to gasp. A second property was that, like the ancient ethyl chloride, it was the quickest acting anesthetic known.

The man by the callboard saw Calhoun. His nostrils caught the odor of dextrethyl. He gasped.

He fell unconscious.

Calhoun waited patiently until the dextrethyl was out of the way. It was almost unique among vapors in that at room temperature it was lighter than air. It rose toward the ceiling. Presently Calhoun moved forward and brought out the polysulphate injector. He bent over the unconscious man. He did not touch him otherwise.

He turned and walked out of the room with Murgatroyd piously marching behind him.

Outside, Calhoun said:

"As one medical man to another, perhaps I shouldn't have done that. But I'm dealing with a health hazard, a plague. Sometimes one has to use psychology to supplement standard measures. I consider that the case here. Anyhow this man should be missed sooner than most. He has a job where his failure to act should be noticed."

"Chee?" asked Murgatroyd zestfully.

"No," said Calhoun. "He won't die. He wouldn't be so unkind."

It was dark outdoors now. When Calhoun stepped out into the street—he'd touched nothing in the callboard office to show that he'd entered it—nightfall was complete. Stars shone brightly, but the empty, unlighted ways of the city were black. There seemed to be a formless menace in the air. When Calhoun moved down the street, Murgatroyd, who hated the dark, reached up a furry paw and held on to Calhoun's hand for reassurance.

Calhoun moved silently and Murgatroyd's footfalls were inaudible. The feel of the never-lived-in city was appalling. A sleeping city seems ghostly and strange, even with lighted streets. An abandoned city is intolerably desolate, with all its inhabitants gone or dead. But a city which has never lived, which lies lifeless under a night sky because its people never came to occupy it—that city has the worst feeling of all. It seems unnatural. It seems insane. It is like a corpse which could have lived but never acquired a soul, and now waits horribly for something demoniac to enter it and give it a seeming of life too horrifying to imagine.

The invaders unquestionably felt that creeping atmosphere of horror. Presently there was proof. Calhoun heard small, drunken noises in the street. He tracked them cautiously. He found the place—one lighted ground-floor window on a long street lined on both sides with towering structures reaching for the sky. The sheer walls were utterly dark. The narrow lane of stars that could be seen overhead seemed utterly remote. The street itself was empty and dark, and murmurous with echoes of sounds that had not ever really been made. And here there were no natural sounds at all. Building walls cut off the normal night sounds of the open country. There was a dead and muffled and murmurous stillness fit to crack one's eardrums.

Except for the drunken singing. Men drank together in an unnecessarily small room, which they had lighted very brightly to try to make it seem alive. All about them was deadness and stillness, so they made supposedly festive noises, priming themselves to cheerfulness with many bottles. With enough to drink, perhaps, the illusion could be believed in. But it was a pitifully tiny thread of sound in a dark and empty city. Outside, where Calhoun and Murgatroyd paused to listen, the noise of drunken singing had a quality of biting irony.

Calhoun grunted, and the sound echoed endlessly between the stark walls around and above.

"We could use those characters," he said coldly, "only there are too many of them."

He and Murgatroyd went on. He'd familiarized himself with the stars, earlier, and knew that he moved in the direction of the landing grid. He'd arranged for one man on duty—at the callboard—to fail to do his work. The process was carefully chosen. He'd knocked out the invader with vortex rings of dextrethyl vapor, and then had given him a shot of polysulphate. The combination was standard, like magnesium sulphate and ether, centuries before. Polysulphate was an assisting anesthetic, never used alone because a man who was knocked out by it stayed out for days. In surgery it was used in a quantity which seemed not to affect a man at all, yet the least whiff of dextrethyl would then put him under for an operation, while he could instantly be revived. It was safer and under better control than any other kind of anesthesia.

But Calhoun had reversed the process. He'd put the callboard operator under with vapor, and then given polysulphate to keep him under for sixty hours or more. And then he'd left him. When the invader was found unconscious, it would bother the other butchers very much. They'd never suspect his condition to be the result of enemy action. They'd consider him in a coma. A coma was the last effect of the plague that had presented them with a planet. They'd believe their fellow to be dying of the plague they were supposed to be immune to. They would panic, expecting immediate death for themselves. But more than one man in a coma-like state would be more effective in producing complete disorganization and despair.

A door banged, back by the lighted window in the desolate black street. Someone came out. Someone else. A third man. They moved along the street, singing hoarsely and untunefully and with words as slurred and uncertain as their footsteps. Echoes resounded between the high building walls. The effect was eerie.

Calhoun moved into a doorway. He waited. When the three men were opposite him, they linked arms to steady themselves. One man roared out quite unprintable verses of a song in which another joined uncertainly from time to time. The third protested aggrievedly. He halted, and the three of them argued solemnly about something indefinable, swaying as they talked with owlish, drunken gravity.

Calhoun lifted the paint-gun. He held down the trigger. Invisible rings of dextrethyl vapor whisked toward the trio. They gasped. They collapsed. Calhoun took his measures.

Presently one man lay unconscious on the street in a coma which imitated perfectly, except for the emaciation, the terminal coma of the fugitives from the city. Some distance away Calhoun plodded on toward the landing grid with a second man, also unconscious, over his shoulder. Murgatroyd followed closely. The third man, stripped to his underwear, waited where he might be found within the next day or two.

CHAPTER SIX

"It is improper to use the term 'gambler' of a man who uses actuarial tables or tables of probability to make wagers which ensure him a favorable percentage of returns. Still less is it proper to call a man who cheats a gambler. He eliminates chance from his operations by his cheating. He does not gamble at all.

'The only true gambler is one who takes risks without considering chance; who acts upon reason or intuition or hunch or superstition without advertising to probability. He ignores the fact that chance as well as thought has a share in determining the outcome of any action. In this sense, the criminal is the true gambler. He is always confident that probability will not interfere; that no random happening will occur. To date, however, there has been no statistical analysis of a crime which has proved it an action which a reasonably prudent man would risk. The effects of pure, random happen-chance can be so overwhelming..."

Probability and Human Conduct—Fitzgerald

THE NIGHT NOISES of the planet Maris III came from all the open space beyond the city itself. From the buildings themselves, of course, there was only silence. There were park areas left between them here and there, and green spaces bordered all the highways. But only small chirping sounds came from the city. The open country sang to the stars.

Calhoun settled himself, with an unconscious burden and Murgatroyd. He could not know how long it would be before the callboard operator would be missed and checked on. He was sure, though, that the appearance of terminal coma in a man who should be immune to the plague would produce results. The callboard man would be brought to the microbiologist who must be in charge of this operation murder. There had to be such a man. He had to know all about the plague. He had to be able to meet any peculiarity that came up. At a guess, only the best qualified of all the men who'd worked to develop the plague would be trusted with its first field test. He might even be the man who himself had devised the synergic combination. He'd be on hand. He'd have every possible bit of equipment he could need, in a superlatively arranged laboratory on the ship. And the callboard man would be brought to him.

Calhoun waited. He had another man in seeming coma, ready for use when the time came. Now he rested in the deep star-shadow of one of the landing grid's massive supports. Murgatroyd stayed close to him. The *tormal* was normally active by day. Darkness daunted him. He tended to whimper if he could not be close to Calhoun.

Overhead loomed the soaring, heavy arches of the landing grid. The grid should handle twenty-thousand-ton liners, and heavier ones too. It was designed to conduct the interstellar business of a world. Beyond it, the city reared up against the stars. The control building, from which the grid was operated, sprawled over half an acre, not far from where Calhoun lay in wait. His eyes were adjusted to the darkness, and he could see faint glows as if there were lighted windows facing away from him. He was within a hundred yards of the giant, globular ship which had brought the Invaders here to do their work of butchery.

There was quiet save for the chorus of myriads of small voices which serenaded the heavens. It was a remarkable total sound. Now and again Calhoun heard sustained deep-bass notes, like the lowest possible tones of a great organ. Then there were liquid trillings, which might come from any kind of bird or beast or reptile. In between came chirpings and abrupt paeans of music, like woodwinds essaying tentative melodic runs.

It was easy for Calhoun to wait. The whole affair had added itself up in his mind. He felt that he not only knew what had happened on this world, but what might happen elsewhere if this particular enterprise proved profitable.

This world of Maris III was to have been a daughter-planet of the old, long-settled Dettra Two. There would have been a close linkage of interest and traditions between the two worlds. They would have had a common tradition, and common blood, and all the ties that can keep two civilizations akin. The older culture had built a city and farms and facilities for half a million of its more adventurous members. They would have come here and entered upon and possessed this world, and they would have zestfully begun its development in the image of the older planet. They would have proudly begun payment for what they had received, and even more proudly prepared to receive more and more and yet more of the senior world's crowded people.

All this was in accord with natural law, which not only determines the courses of worlds about their central suns, but dictates what is wise and fit and suitable for mankind. But men need not heed the laws of nature. They cannot be changed, but they can be broken. And somewhere there was a world, or at least the government of a world, which essayed to break the laws Calhoun knew were essential.

In the great cosmos even crime is matter-of-fact. Natural laws can be twisted to aid it. For example, a spaceship could be built with wings. In space they would not matter. Normally they would be useless. But if somebody wanted to commit a very great crime, a spaceship could be built with wings, and instead of entering atmosphere on rockets designed only to let it down gently in case of emergency, it could enter an unsuspecting planet's air and fly there on the wings it had brought through light-years of emptiness.

Such a winged spacecraft, flying by rocket power as an airplane, could dump out frozen pellets of contagion. It could choose a place for this dumping which was upwind from a city, and it could choose a height so that an area of many, many square miles would be saturated with invisible, deadly creators of disease. The ship could even flyaway and up and up and up, and ultimately depend on its rockets alone in airlessness to take it up to where its spacedrive could operate in unstressed space. It could return to its home in overdrive, and the only sign of its coming anywhere—the only sign that would be known—would be a memory of thunder rolling in a star-filled sky. But later there would be a plague.

Exactly this had happened here. The empty city had been drenched with virus particles so tiny that only electron microscopes could tell that they existed, and could not tell them from others closely kin to them. But they were deadly. Singly, no. Alone, each of two types might produce only the most trivial of infections. Combined, they produced a toxin which took from human blood its power to carry oxygen. In a sense, the effect was like that of carbon monoxide. More directly, they caused bodies to starve for oxygen.

And all this was unnatural. Men had devised the plague and the means of spreading it. They made use of it. On the world where thunder had rolled in a cloudless sky, men and women died. Presently a ship came to verify it, to make sure that everything went wrong on Maris III. They knew the plague could not harm them. They murdered the few survivors in the city that they could find. They hunted down the others in the open country.

They now waited for more of their own kind to come, to occupy the planet made ready for them. When ships came from Dettra Two, which had built the city and prepared the fields, the settlers then in occupation could refuse to let them land. Or they could let them land and then watch them die. Maris III was useless now to the world that had developed it. Only the world that had murdered its first small population could have any benefit from it at all. Because, of course, the emigrants from the criminal world could be immunized to the plague their rulers had sent before them. They could live there freely, like the butchers who came first of all. It might seem a very brilliant course of conduct.

But Calhoun ground his teeth. He could see other angles to this affair. Men who could arrange this could go further. Much further. What he'd imagined was trivial compared to what could come next.

There was a light in motion in the city. Calhoun sat up, all alertness, to watch it. It was a ground-car on a highway, headlights glaring to light the way before it. It vanished behind buildings. It reappeared. It crossed a far-flung bridge and vanished again, and again reappeared. It was drawing closer, and presently its lights glared in Calhoun's eyes as it sped furiously across the landing grid's turf floor, headed for the sprawling building where the transformers and the controls for the grid were housed.

There it came to a swiftly braked stop. Its lights stayed on. Men jumped from it and ran into the control building. Calhoun heard no voices. The songs of the night creatures would have blotted out human voices. In minutes, though, more men came out of the building. They clustered about the ground-car. After only seconds, the car was again in motion, jouncing and bouncing over the turf toward the grounded spaceship.

It stopped within a hundred yards of where Calhoun had concealed himself. The headlights glittered and glistened against the bulging, silvery metal of the spacecraft. A man shouted at it:

"Open up! Open up! Something's happened! A man's sick! It looks like the plague!"

There was no sign. He shouted again. Another man pounded on the thick metal of the airlock's outer door.

A voice spoke suddenly out of external loud-speakers.

"What's this? What's the matter?"

Many voices tried to babble, but a harsh voice silenced them and barked statements, every one of which Calhoun could have written down in advance. There'd been a man on watch in the city's communication center. He didn't put through calls from different places in use by the invaders. Someone went to find out why. The man at the callboard was unconscious. It looked like he had the plague. It looked like the shots he'd had to make him immune didn't work.

The voice coming over the loud-speakers said:

"Nonsense! Bring him in!"

Seconds later the airlock door cracked open and descended outward, making a ramp from the ground to the cubbyhole which was the lock as now revealed. The men on the ground hauled a limp figure out of the ground-car. They half-carried and half-dragged it up the ramp into the lock. Calhoun saw the inner door open. They dragged the figure inside.

Then nothing happened, except that one man came out almost immediately, wiping his hands on his uniform as if hysterically afraid that by touching his unconscious companion he'd infected himself with the plague.

Presently another man came out. He trembled. Then the others. The harsh voice said savagely:

"So he's got to find out what's the matter. It *can't* be the plague. We had shots against it. It's bound to be all right. Maybe he fainted or something. Stop acting like you're going to die! Go back on duty! I'll order a roll call, just in case."

Calhoun listened with satisfaction. The inner airlock door closed, but the outer one remained down as a ramp. The car trundled away, stopped and discharged some passengers at the control building, and went off into the distance. It disappeared on the highway where it had first appeared.

"The man I knocked out," he said dryly to Murgatroyd, "impresses them unfavorably. They hope he's only an accident. We'll see. But that authoritative person is going to order a roll call. He ought to find something to bother them all, when that takes place."

"Chee," said Murgatroyd in a subdued tone.

There was again silence and stillness save for the open country song to the stars. There seemed to be occasional drumbeats in that chorus now.

It was half an hour before light showed on the ground by the control building. It was as if invisible doors had been opened, and light streamed out of them. In minutes a traveling light appeared. It vanished and was again visible, like the lights of the first car.

"Ha!" said Calhoun, gratified. "Checking up, they found the invader we left in the street. They reported it by communicator. Maybe they reported two others missing—one of whom is beside you, Murgatroyd. They ought to feel slightly upset."

The car dashed across the landing grid's center and braked. Figures waited for it. With the briefest of pauses it came again to the ship with the opened airlock door. The harsh voice panted:

"Here's another one! We're bringing him in."

The loud-speaker said, somehow vexed:

"Very well. But the first man hasn't got the plague. His metabolic rate is normal. He has not got the plague!"

"Here's another one, just the same!"

The figures struggled up the ramp with a second limp burden. Minutes later they emerged again.

"He didn't get that first man awake," said an uneasy voice. "That looks bad to me."

"He says it ain't the plague."

"If he says it's not," snapped the authoritative voice, "then it's not! He ought to know. He invented the plague!"

Calhoun, behind the giant support for the landing grid, said, "Ah…" very quietly to himself.

"But—look here," said a frightened voice. "There were doctors in the city when we got here. Maybe some of 'em got away. Maybe—maybe they had some kinda germ that they've turned loose to kill us…"

The authoritative voice snarled. All the voices broke into a squabbling babble. The invaders were worried. They were frightened. Normally it would never have occurred to them to suspect a disease deliberately introduced among them. But they were here to follow up just such a disease. They did not understand such menaces. They'd been willing enough to profit, so long as the matter was strictly one-sided. But now it looked like some disease was striking them down. It seemed very probable that it was the plague to which they had been assured that they were immune. Some of them already had the shakes.

The car went away from the grounded spaceship. It stopped for a long time before the control building. There was agitated argument there. Calhoun heard the faint squabbling sound above the voices of the night. The car went away again.

He allowed twenty minutes to pass. They seemed very long to him. Then he picked up the man he'd knocked out, outside the room with the noisy drinking party. He heaved him over his shoulder. He'd pulled the uniform of the third of his dark-street victims over his own, and that third man lay in an areaway in his underwear. He'd be found eventually.

"We'll ask for our invitation into the ship—and the laboratory, Murgatroyd. Come along!"

He moved toward the still and silent spaceship.

It swelled and loomed enormously as he approached it. The outside lock door still lay extended downward as a ramp. He tramped up on the metal incline. He went into the lock. There he banged on the inner door and called:

"Here's another one! Out like the others! What'll I do with him?"

There'd be microphones in the lock, as there were outside. But his voice wouldn't go so loudly to the control building. He could not plausibly moderate his tone. He made it agitated.

"Here's a third man, out like the others! What'll I do with him?"

A metallic voice said angrily:

"Wait!"

Calhoun waited. Two unconscious men, brought separately by a group of men who were more frightened the second time than the first, made it extremely likely that a third unconscious man would not have a group of solicitous companions with him. One man to risk the supposed contagion was very much more likely.

He heard footsteps beyond the inner lock door. It opened. A voice rasped:

"Bring him in!"

He turned his back, this man who had come down to the airlock to spring the catch of the inner door. Calhoun followed him inside the ship, with Murgatroyd trodding fearfully between his feet. The lock door clicked shut. The figure in the white lab coat went trudging on ahead. It was a small figure. It limped a little. It was not well-shaped.

Calhoun, with an unconscious member of the invading party used as a drape to hide his paint-gun—so suitable a weapon, as it had turned out up to now—followed after him. He listened grimly for any sound which would indicate any other human being inside the space ship. Now that he had seen—even from behind—the figure of the field director of the project to exterminate the proper inhabitants of Maris III, he coldly reasoned that there would probably not be even a laboratory assistant.

The queer figure moving before him fitted in a specific niche. There are people who, because they are physically unattractive, become personalities. All too many girls—and men, too—do not bother to become anything but good to look at. Some people who are not good to look at accept the situation courageously and become people who are good to know. But others rebel bitterly.

Knowing, as he did, that this man had used brains and skill and tedious labor to devise a method of mass murder, Calhoun felt almost able to write his biography. He had been grotesque. He hated those who found him grotesque. He dreamed grandiose dreams of gaining power so that he could punish those he envied and hated. He put into his schemes for revenge against a cosmos that gave him scorn, all the furious energy that could have been used in other ways. He would develop an astounding patience and an incredible venom. He would scheme and scheme and scheme...

Calhoun had met people who could have chosen this way. One of the great men at Sector Headquarters, whose praise was more valued than fine gold, was odd to look at when you first glimpsed him. But you never noticed it after five minutes. There was a planetary president in Cygnus, a teacher on Cetis Alpha, a musician... Calhoun could think of many. But the hobbling figure before him hadn't chosen to follow the natural law, which advises courage. He'd chosen hate instead, and frustration was inevitable.

Into the laboratory. Here Murgatroyd cheered. This place was brightly lighted. Gleaming instruments were familiar. Even the smells of a beautifully equipped biological laboratory were reassuring and homelike to Murgatroyd. He said happily:

"Chee-chee-chee!"

The small figure whirled. Dark eyes widened and glared. Calhoun slipped his burden to the floor. His Med Service uniform appeared beneath the invader's tunic as the downward-sliding body tugged at the cloth.

"I'm sorry," said Calhoun gently, "but I have to put you under arrest for violating the basic principles of public health. Contriving and spreading a lethal plague amounts to at least that."

The figure whirled. It snatched. Then it darted toward Calhoun, desperately trying to use a surgeon's scalpel, the only deadly weapon within reach.

Calhoun pressed the trigger of the vortex-ring apparatus which was designed to paint the walls of buildings. Only this one didn't have paint in it. It shot invisible vortex rings of dextrethyl vapor instead.

CHAPTER SEVEN

"In one perfectly real sense, all motives and all satisfactions are subjective. After all, we do live in our own skulls. But a man can do something he wishes to do and then contemplate the consequences of his action with pleasure. This pleasure, be sure, is subjective, but it is directly related to reality and to the objective cosmos about him. However, there is an ultra subjective type of motivation and satisfaction which is of great importance in human conduct. Many persons find their greatest satisfaction in contemplating themselves in some particular context. Such people find apparently complete satisfaction in a dramatic gesture, in a finely stated aspiration, or simply in a mere pretense of significance or wisdom or worth. The objective results of such gestures or pretenses are rarely considered. Very often great hardship and suffering and even deaths have been brought about by some person who raptly contemplated the beautiful drama of his behavior, and did not even think of its consequences to someone else..."

Probability and Human Conduct—Fitzgerald

CALHOUN MADE the small man helpless with the invader's' uniform he'd pulled over his own, and now tore it into strips. He was painstaking about the job. He tied his captive in a chair, and then encased him in a veritable cocoon of cloth strips. Then he examined the laboratory.

Murgatroyd strutted as Calhoun went over the equipment. Most of it was totally familiar. There were culture trays, visual and electron microscopes, autoclaves and irradiation apparatus, pipettes and instruments for microanalysis, thermostatic cabinets capable of keeping culture material within the hundredth of a degree of desired temperature. Murgatroyd was completely at home now.

Presently Calhoun heard a gasp. He turned and nodded to his prisoner.

"How-do," he said politely. "I've been very much interested in your work. I'm Med Service, by the way. I came here to do a routine planetary health-check and somebody tried to kill me when I called for landing coordinates. They'd have done better to let me land and then blast me when I came out of my ship. The other was the more dramatic gesture, of course."

Dark, beady eyes regarded him. They changed remarkably from moment to moment. At one instant they were filled with a flaming fury which was practically madness. At another they seemed to grow cunning. Yet again they showed animal-like fear.

Calhoun said detachedly:

"I doubt that there's any use in talking to you now. I'll wait until you have the situation figured out. I'm in the ship. There appears to be nobody else in a condition to start any trouble. The two men your—ah—mop-up party brought here are out for some days." He added explanatorily, "Polysulphate. An overdose. It's so simple I didn't think you'd guess it. I knocked them out so you'd be ready to let me in with a third specimen."

The mummy-like bound figure made inarticulate noises. There was the sound of grinding teeth. There were bubbling sounds of crazy, frustrated rage.

"You're in a state of emotional shock," said Calhoun. "I guess that part is real and part is faked. I'll leave you alone to get over it. I want some information. I think you'll want to bargain. I'll leave you alone to work it out."

He went out of the laboratory. He felt an acute distaste for the man he'd captured. It was true that he believed the small man had received an acute emotional shock on finding himself captured and helpless. But a part of that shock would be rage so horrible as to threaten madness. Calhoun guessed coldly that anyone who had made the decision and lived the life he ascribed to the bound man—his guess, as it happened, was remarkably exact—could literally be goaded to death or madness, now that he was bound and could be taunted at will. It happened that he did not want to taunt his prisoner.

He went over the ship. He checked its type and design, verified the spaceyard in which it had been built, made an exact list in his own mind of what would be needed to make it into an inert hulk of no use to anybody, and then went back to the laboratory.

His prisoner panted, exhausted. There were very minor stretchings of the cloth strips which held him. Calhoun matter-of-factly made them tight again. His prisoner spat unspeakable, hysterical curses at him.

"Good," said Calhoun, unmoved. "Get the madness out of your system and we'll talk."

He moved to leave the laboratory again. A voice came out of a loud-speaker, and he instantly searched for and found the microphone by which it could be answered. He flicked it off as his prisoner tried to scream commands into it.

"Haven't you found out yet?" asked the loudspeaker apprehensively. *"Don't you know what's the matter with those men? There are two more missing on roll call. There's something like panic building up. The men are guessing that a native doctor's spreading a plague among us!"*

Calhoun shrugged. The voice came from outside. It had been an authoritative voice, not long since. Now it was a badly worried one. He did not answer its questions. It repeated them. It waited and asked again. It almost pleaded for a reply. With the microphone off, however, there could be none. Calhoun listened detachedly when the authoritative voice, which must be that of the commander of the butchers, grew resentful at being ignored. It faded out, trembling, shaking a little, but whether with hatred or terror he could not be sure. It could be either.

"Your popularity's diminishing," said Calhoun. He put down the microphone, safely off. He noted a spacephone receiver alongside the speaker-amplifier. "Hmmm," he said. "Suspicious, eh? You didn't even trust the skipper. Had to do your own receiving. Typical!"

The trussed-up, wizened man spoke suddenly with absolute cold precision.

"What do you want?" he demanded.

"Information," said Calhoun.

"For yourself? What do you want? I can give it to you!" said the mouth beneath the half-mad dark eyes. "I can give you anything you can imagine! I can give you riches more than you can dream!"

Calhoun sat negligently on the arm of a chair.

"I'll listen," he observed. "But apparently you're only technical director of the operation here. It's not a very big operation. You'd only a thousand people to kill. You're acting under orders. How could you give me anything important?"

"This—" His prisoner cursed. "This is a test—an experiment! Let me go, let it be finished, and I can give you a world to rule. I'll make you king of a planet! You'll have millions of slaves! You'll have women by hundreds or thousands if you choose!"

Calhoun said detachedly, "You wouldn't expect me to believe that without the details."

The dark eyes flamed. Then, with an effort of will that was as violent as his rage had been, the small bound figure brought itself to composure. It was not calmness. Fury surged up when he attempted a persuasive gesture and could not move. Frustration maddened him to panting for breath. But between such moments, he talked with a terrifying plausibility, with a precision of detail that showed a scheme worked out with infinite care. It was *his* scheme. He had convinced a planetary government to try it. He was necessary to it. He would have power to spare and he could bribe Calhoun with everything that was rich and alluring and apparently irresistible. He set persuasively to work to bribe him.

It was quite horrible.

First there had to be explanation, in such detail that a Med Service man could know that his bribes would infallibly be available and could not fail.

The taking over of Maris III was, as Calhoun had more than guessed, a mere field trial of a new method for interplanetary war and conquest. Here was a new planet. It had a small caretaker population waiting for the hundreds of thousands of permanent inhabitants due to take over its ready-built city and roads and farms. It had been used for the testing of a new and irresistible kind of conquest. Plague! Plague had been rained upon its principal and, so far, only city. In the night. The people knew nothing about it. They began to die, and even then did not know why they died or what had caused it or when the cause of their deaths was introduced. They died!

Calhoun nodded. He was not impressed by the mysterious phrasing. It might have been imposing to somebody who had not worked out for himself how the plague had been introduced and what it was and how it had been designed to escape detection by ordinary microbiological methods.

His captive went on. His tone wheedled, and was strident, and in turn was utterly convincing and remarkably persuasive.

Once Maris III was occupied by colonists from the world that had sent the plague, nothing could be done. Dettra Two could never land its people in the city. They would die. Only the usurping population could survive there. For all time to come the world of Maris III must belong to the folk who had planted it with death. The permanent colonists here must be immunized like the members of the invading party themselves.

"Who," said Calhoun, "are not as happy as they used to be."

His captive licked his lips and went on, his eyes deadly and his tone reasonable and seductive and remarkably hypnotic.

But Maris III was only a test. Once the process was proved here, there were other worlds to be taken over. Not only new colony-worlds like this. Old and established worlds would find themselves attacked by plagues their doctors would be helpless to combat. Then there would come ships from the world that had tried out its technique on Maris III. The ships could end the plagues. They would prove it. They would offer to sell life to all the citizens of the dying worlds—at a price.

"Unprofessional," said Calhoun, "but probably profitable."

The price, in effect, would be submission. It would amount to slavery. Those who would not accept the bargain would die.

"Of course," said Calhoun, "they might try to back out of such a bargain later."

His captive smiled a thin-lipped smile, while his eyes did not change at all. He explained convincingly that if there was a revolt, it would not matter. The countermeasure to a new defiance would always be a new plague. There were many plagues ready to use. They would build an interstellar empire in which rebellion would be a form of suicide. No world once taken over could ever free itself. No world once chosen could possibly resist. There would be worlds by tens and scores and hundreds, to be ruled by men like Calhoun. He would rate a planet kingdom of his own. His Med Service training entitled him to an empire! He would be absolute ruler and absolute master of millions of abject slaves who must please his most trivial whim or die!

"An objection," said Calhoun. "You haven't mentioned the Med Service. I don't think it would take kindly to such a system of planetary conquest."

Here was the highest test of the prisoner's ability to sway and persuade and convince and almost to hypnotize. He had in a matter of minutes to make the Med Service ridiculous, and to point out the defenselessness of its Sector Headquarters, and then—without arousing ancient prejudices—to make it seem natural and inevitable and almost humorous that Med Service Sector Headquarters would receive special precautionary fusion-bomb treatment as soon as the Maris III task was finished. Calhoun stirred. His prisoner spoke even more urgently, more desperately. He pictured worlds on which every living being would be Calhoun's slave—

"That'll do," said Calhoun. "I've got the information I wanted."

"Then release me," said his prisoner eagerly. And then his burning eyes read Calhoun's no-longer-guarded expression.

"You accept," he cried fiercely. "You accept! You *can't* refuse! *You can't!*"

"Of course I can," said Calhoun annoyedly. "You've no idea! I wouldn't want a million slaves, or even one. I'm reasonably sane! And such a crazy scheme couldn't work anyhow. Sheer probability would throw in so many unfavorable chance happenings that it would be bound to go smash. I'm proof of it. I'm an unfavorable chance happening right here, the very first time you try the beastly business!"

His prisoner tried to talk more persuasively still. He tried to be more tempting still. He tried, but his throat clicked. He struggled to be more convincing and more alluring than it was possible to be. Suddenly he shrieked curses at Calhoun. They were horrible to listen to. He screamed—

Calhoun raised the paint-gun, his features twisted and wry. He sent a single small vortex ring.

In the sudden silence that fell, a tiny, tinny voice sounded from the spacephone receiver at one side of the laboratory.

"Calling ground," said a voice faintly. *"Ship from home with passengers calling ground on Maris III. Calling ground…"*

Calhoun jerked his head about and listened to the reiterated call. Then he bent to the necessary next thing to be done with his prisoner.

"Calling ground," said the voice patiently. *"We do not read you. If you are answering, we do not pick up your signal. We will go in orbit and continue to call. Calling ground…"*

Calhoun turned it off. Murgatroyd said inquiringly:

"Chee?"

"That's a deadline," said Calhoun grimly. "For us. It's a shipload of happy, immunized colonists, ready to land here. We blew the landing grid, Murgatroyd, when they tried to butter us over the inside of the Med Ship. Apparently we blew their spacephone at the same time. So the spacephone in this ship, here is the only one working. And we have too much sense to answer that call. But it gives us a deadline, just the same. If they still don't raise their friends, the ship may stay in orbit, but somebody'll come down in a lifeboat to find out what's wrong. And that will shoot the works! We'll have a passenger ship full of enthusiasts ready to land and finish the mopping-up business—and us! There's just you and me, Murgatroyd, to take care of the situation. Let's get at it!"

But it was very close to dawn when he and Murgatroyd left the grounded ship. Calhoun grimaced when he saw the vast crimson glory of approaching sunrise in the sky to the east. He saw a ground-car before the building in which the landing grid controls were housed.

"Worked up like these characters are," said Calhoun, "and suspecting somebody of spreading plagues for them to catch, they won't be cordial to anybody who didn't come here with them. I don't like the idea of trying simply to walk away when there's all this daylight. I think we'd better try to take that car, Murgatroyd. Come along!"

He headed for the control building. Judging by the night before, the occupied rooms had no windows facing toward the landed spacecraft. But he moved cautiously from one great arch-foundation to the next. When he'd reached the last possible bit of shelter, however, the ground-car was still fifty yards away.

"We run for it," he told Murgatroyd.

He and the tiny *tormal* bolted through the rosy dawnlight. They had covered thirty yards when someone came out of the control building. He moved toward the ground-car. He heard Calhoun's pelting footsteps on the turf. He turned. For one instant he stared. Calhoun was a stranger. There should be no living strangers on this planet—they should all be dead. Here was an explanation of two men found unconscious and probably dying, and two more missing. The invader roared. His blaster came out.

Calhoun fired first. The snarling rasp of a blaster is unmistakable. The invader's weapon burst thunderously.

"Run!" snapped Calhoun.

Voices. A man peered out a window. Calhoun was a stranger with a blaster in his hand. The sight of him was a challenge to murder. The man in the window yelled. As Calhoun snapped a shot at him he jerked inside and the window crackled and smoked where the blaster charge hit.

Man and *tormal* reached the line of the ground-car and the building door. The door was open. Calhoun swung up the sprayer and pumped explosive dextrethyl vapor into the room in a stream of vortex rings. He backed toward the ground-car, with Murgatroyd dancing agitatedly about his feet.

There was a crash of glass. Somebody'd plunged out a window. There were rushing feet inside. They'd be racing toward the door, from inside. But the hallway, or whatever was immediately inside, would be filled with anesthetic gas. Men would gasp and fall.

A man did fall. Calhoun heard the crash of his body as it hit the floor. But another man came plunging around the building's corner, blaster out, searching for Calhoun. He had to sight his target though, and then aim for it. Calhoun had only to pull his trigger. He did.

More shouting inside the building. More rushing feet. More falls. Then there was the beginning of the rasping snarl of a blaster, and finally a cushioned, booming, roaring detonation which was the ignited dextrethyl vapor. The blast lifted part of the building's roof. It shattered partitions. It blew out windows.

Calhoun backed toward the ground-car. A blaster bolt flashed past him. He deliberately traversed the building with his trigger held down. Smoke and flame leaped up. At least one more invader crumpled. Calhoun heard a voice yelling:

"We're being attacked! The natives are throwing bombs! Rally! Rally! We need help!"

It would be a broadcast call for assistance. Wherever men idled or loafed or tried desultorily to find something to loot, they would hear it. Even the crew working to repair the landing grid—and they would be close by—would hear it and swarm to help. Hunters would come. Men in cars—

Calhoun snatched Murgatroyd to the seat beside him. He turned the ignition key and tires screamed as he shot away.

CHAPTER EIGHT

"It has to be recognized that man is a social animal in the same sense, though in a different manner, that ants and bees are social creatures. For an ant city to prosper, there have to be natural laws to protect it against unfavorable actions on the part of its members. It is not enough to speak of instincts to prevent antisocial actions. There are mutations of instinct as well as of form, in ants as in other creatures. It is not enough even to speak of social pressure, which among ants would be an impulse to destroy deviant members of the community. There are natural laws to protect an ant city against the instinct-control which would destroy it, as well as against the abandonment of instincts or actions necessary to the ant city as a whole. There are, in short, natural laws and natural forces which protect societies against their own members. In human society..."

Probability and Human Conduct—Fitzgerald

THE HIGHWAYS were, of course, superb. The car raced forward, and its communicator began to chatter as somebody in the undamaged part of the grid-control building announced hysterically that a stranger had killed men and gotten away in a car. It described its course. It commanded that he be headed off. It shrilly demanded that he be killed, killed, killed!

Another voice took over. This voice was curt and coldly furious. It snapped precise instructions.

And Calhoun found himself on a gracefully curving, rising road. It soared, and he was midway between towers when another car flashed toward him. He took his blaster in his left hand. In the spilt second during which the cars passed each other, he blasted it. There was a monstrous surge of smoke and flame as the stricken car's Duhanne cell shorted and vaporized half the metal of the car itself.

There came other voices. Somebody had sighted the explosion. The voice in the communicator roared for silence.

"You," he rasped. *"If you got him, report yourself!"*

"Chee-chee-chee!" chattered Murgatroyd excitedly.

But Calhoun did not report.

"He got one of us," raged the icy voice. *"Get ahead of him and blast him!"*

Calhoun's car went streaking down the far side of the traffic bridge. It rounded a curve on two wheels. It flashed between two gigantic empty buildings and came to a side road, and plunged into that, and came again to a division and took the left-hand turn, and next time took the right. But the muttering voices continued in the communicator. One of the invaders was ordered to the highest possible bridge from which he could watch all lower-level roadways. Others were to post themselves here and there—and to stay still! A group of four cars was coming out of the storage building. Blast any single car in motion. Blast it! And report, report, report!

"I suspect," said Calhoun to the agitated Murgatroyd beside him, "that this is what is known as military tactics. If they ring us in... There aren't but so many of them, though. The trick for us is to get out of the city. We need more choices for action. So—"

The communicator panted a report of his sighting, from a cobweb-like bridge at the highest point of the city. He was heading—

He changed his heading. He had so far seen but one of his pursuers' cars. Now he went racing along empty, curving highways, among untenanted towers and between balconied walls with blank-eyed windows gazing at him everywhere.

It was nightmarish because of the magnificence and the emptiness of the city all about him. He plunged along graceful highways, across delicately arched bridges, through crazy ramifications of its lesser traffic arteries—and he saw no motion anywhere. The wind whistled past the car windows, and the tires sang a high-pitched whine, and the sun shone down and small clouds floated tranquilly in the sky. There were no signs of life or danger anywhere on the splendid highways or in the beautiful buildings. Only voices muttered in the communicator of the car. He'd been seen here, flashing around a steeply banked curve. He'd swerved from a waiting ambush by pure chance. He'd—

He saw green to the left. He dived down a sloping ramp toward one of the smaller park-areas of the city.

And as he came from between the stone guard-rails of the road, the top of the car exploded over his head. He swerved and roared into dense shrubbery, jerked Murgatroyd free despite the *tormal's* clinging fast with all four paws and his tail, and dived into the underbrush. Somehow, instinctively, he clung to the vortex-gun.

He ran, with his free hand plucking solidified droplets of hot metal from his garments and his flesh. They hurt abominably. But the man who'd fired wouldn't believe he'd missed, followed as his blasting was by the instant wrecking of the car. That man would report success before he moved in to view the corpse of his supposed victim. But there'd be other cars coming. At the moment it was necessary for Calhoun to get elsewhere, fast.

He heard the rushing sound of arriving cars while he panted and sweated through the foliage of the park. He reached the far side and a road, and on beyond there was a low stone wall. He knew instantly what it was. Service highways ran in cuts, for the most part roofed over to hide them from sight, but now and again open to the sky for ventilation. He'd entered the city by one of them. Here was another. He swung himself over the wall and dropped. Murgatroyd recklessly and excitedly followed.

It was a long drop, and he staggered when he landed. He heard a soft rushing noise above. A car raced past. Instants later, another.

Limping, Calhoun ran to the nearest service gate. He entered and closed it. Scorched and aching, he climbed to the echoing upper stories of this building. Presently he looked out. His car had been wrecked in one of the smaller park areas of the city. Now there were other cars at two-hundred-yard intervals all about it. It was believed that he was in the brushwood somewhere. Besides the cars of the cordon, there were now twenty men on foot receiving orders from an authoritative figure in their midst.

They scattered. Twenty yards apart, they began to move across the park. Other men arrived and strengthened the cordon toward which he was supposed to be driven. A fly could not have escaped.

Those who marched across the park began methodically to burn it to ashes before them with their blasters.

Calhoun watched. Then he remembered something and was appalled. Two days before while he was among the fugitives in the glade, Kim Walpole had asked hungrily if they whose lives he had saved could not do something to help him. And he'd said that if they saw the smoke of a good-sized fire in the city they might investigate. He'd had not the faintest intention of calling on them. But they might see this cloud of smoke and believe he wanted them to come and help!

"Damn!" he said wryly to Murgatroyd. "After all, there's a limit to any one series of actions with probable favorable chance consequences. I'd better start a new one. We might have whittled the invaders down and made the rest run away, but I had to start using a car! And that led to the chance making of a fire! So now we start all over with a new policy."

He explored the building quickly. He prepared his measures. He went back to the window from which he'd looked. He cracked it open.

He opened fire with his blaster. The range was long, but with the beam cut down to minimum spread he'd knocked over a satisfying number of the men below before they swarmed toward the building, sending before them a barrage of blaster fire that shattered the windows and had the stone facade smoking furiously.

"This," said Calhoun, "is an occasion where we have to change their advantage in numbers and weapons into an unfavorable circumstance for them. They'll be brave because they're many. Let's go!"

He met four ground-car loads of refugees with his arms in the air. He did not want to be shot down by mistake. He said hurriedly, when Kim and the other lean survivors gathered about him:

"Everything's all right. We've a pack of prisoners but we won't bother to feed them intravenously for the moment. How'd you get the ground-cars?"

"Hunters," said Kim savagely. "We found them and killed them and took their cars. We found some other refugees, too, and I cured them—at least they will be cured soon. When we saw the smoke, we started for the city. Some of us still have the plague, but we've all had our serum shots. And half of us have arms now."

"All of us have arms," said Calhoun, "and to spare. The invaders are quite peacefully sleeping—just about all of them. I did knock over a few with long-range blaster-shots, and they won't wake up. Most of them, though, tried to storm a building from which I'd fired on them. I stood them off a fair length of time, and then ducked after dumping dextrethyl in the air-conditioning system. Murgatroyd and I waited a suitable time and then lengthened their slumber period with polysulfate. I doubt there'll be any more trouble with the butchers. But we've got to get to the spaceship they landed in. I fixed it so it couldn't possibly take off, but there are some calls coming in from space. The only working spacephone here is in the ship. The first load of immunized, enthusiastic colonists are in orbit now, giving the gang aground a little more time to answer. I want you people to talk to them."

"We'll bring their ship down," said the broad-bearded man hungrily, "and blast them as they come out of the port!"

Calhoun shook his head.

"To the contrary," he said mildly. "You'll put on the clothes of some of our prisoners, and you'll let yourselves be seen by the joyous newcomers in their spacephone screen. You'll pretend to be the characters we really have safely sleeping, and you'll say that the plague worked much too well. You'll say it wiped out the original inhabitants—that's you—and then changed into a dozen other plagues and wiped out all the little butcher-boys who came to mop up. You'll give details of the other kinds of plague that the real plague turned into. You'll be pathetic. You'll beg them to land and pick up you four or five dying, multiply diseased, highly contagious survivors. You'll tell them the plague has mutated until even the native animals are dying of it. Flying things fall dead from the air. Chirping things in the trees and grass are wiped out. You'll picture Maris III as a world on which no animal life can hope ever to live again—and you'll beg them to come down and pick you up and take you home with them."

The broad-bearded man stared. Then he said, "But they won't land."

"No," agreed Calhoun. "They won't. They'll go home. Unless the government has them all killed before they can talk, they'll tell their world what happened. They'll be half dead with fear that the immunizing shots they received will mutate and turn them into the kind of plague victims you'll make yourself look like. And just what do you think will happen on the world they came from?"

Kim said hungrily, "They'll kill their rulers. They'll try to do it before they die of the plagues they'll imagine. They'll revolt! If a man has a bellyache he'll go crazy with terror and try to kill a government official because his government has murdered him!"

Kim drew a deep breath. He smiled with no amusement at all.

"I like that," he said with a sort of deadly calm. "I like that very much."

"After all," observed Calhoun, "once an empire had been started, with the subjugated populations kept subdued by a threat of plague, how long would it be before the original population was enslaved by the same threat? Go and invent some interesting plagues and make yourselves look terrifying. Heaven knows you're lean enough! But you can make yourselves look worse. I said, once, that a medical man sometimes has to use psychology in addition to the regular measures against plague. The Med Service will check on that planet presently, but I think its ambition to be a health hazard to the rest of the galaxy will be ended."

"Yes," said Kim. He moved away. Then he stopped. "What about your prisoners? They're knocked out now. What about them?"

Calhoun shrugged. "Oh, we'll let them sleep until we finish repairing the landing grid. I think I can be helpful with that."

"Every one of them is a murderer," growled the broad-bearded man.

"True," agreed Calhoun. "But lynching is bad business. It even offers the possibility of unfavorable chance consequences. Let's take care of the shipload of colonists first."

So they did. It was odd how they could take a sort of pleasure in the enactment of imagined disaster even greater than they had suffered. Their eyes gleamed happily as they went about their task.

The passenger ship went away. It did not have a pleasant journey. When it landed, its passengers burst tumultuously out of the spaceport and told their story. Their home world went into a panic which was the more uncontrollable because the people had been very carefully told how deadly the tamed plagues would be to the inhabitants of worlds that they might want to take over. But now they believed the tamed plagues had turned upon them.

The deaths, especially among members of the ruling class, were approximately equal in number to those a deadly pandemic would have caused.

But back on Maris III things moved smoothly. Rather more than eighty people, altogether, were found and treated and ultimately helped with the matter of the slumbering invaders. That was almost a labor of love. Certainly it gave great satisfaction. The landing grid was back in operation two days after the passenger ship left. They took the landed spaceship and smashed its drive and communicators, and they wrecked its Duhanne cells. They took out the breech-plugs of the rockets and dumped the rocket fuel, saving just enough for the little Med Ship. Naturally, they removed the lifeboats.

And then they revived the unconscious butcher-invaders and put them, one by one, into the spacecraft in which they had come. That craft was now a hulk. It could not drive or use rockets or even signal. Its vision screens were blind; the Med Ship used some of them.

And then they used the landing grid—Calhoun checking the figures—and they put their prisoners up in orbit to await the arrival of proper authority. They could feed themselves, but any attempt at escape would be pure and simple suicide. They could not attempt to escape.

"And now," said Calhoun, when the planet was clean of strangers again, "now I'll bring my ship to the grid. We'll recharge my Duhanne cells and replace my vision screens. I can make it here on rockets, but it's a long way to headquarters. So I'll report, and a field team will come here and check out the planet, artificial plagues included. They'll arrange, somehow, to take care of the prisoners up in orbit. That's not my affair.

Maybe Dettra Two would like to have them. In the meantime, they can search their consciences."

Kim said, frowning:

"You put something over on us! You kept us so busy we forgot one man. You said there'd be a microbiologist in the invaders' party. You said he'd probably be the man who had invented the plague. And he's up there in orbit with the rest—he'll get no more than they get! You put something over on us! He deserves some special treatment!"

Calhoun said very evenly:

"Revenge is always apt to have unfavorable chance consequences. Let him alone. You've no right to punish him. You've only the right to punish a child to correct it, or to punish a man to deter others from doing what he's done. Do you expect to correct the kind of man who'd invent the plague that flourished here, and meant to use it for the making of an empire of slaves? Do you think others need to be deterred from trying the same thing?"

Kim said thickly:

"But he's a murderer! All the murders were his! He deserves—"

"Condign punishment?" asked Calhoun sharply. "You've no right to administer it. Anyhow, think what he's up against!"

"He's—he's..." Kim's face changed. "He's up there in orbit, hopeless, with his butchers all around him and blaming him for the fix they're in. They've nothing to do but hate him. Nothing..."

"You didn't arrange that situation," said Calhoun coldly. "He did. You simply put prisoners in a safe place because it would be impractical to guard them, otherwise. I suggest you forget him."

Kim looked sickish. He shook his head to clear it. He tried to thrust the man who'd planned pure horror out of his mind. He said slowly:

"I wish we could do something for you."

"Put up a statue," said Calhoun dryly, "and in twenty years nobody will know what it was for. You and Helen are going to be married, aren't you?" When Kim nodded, Calhoun said, "In course of time, if you remember and think it worthwhile, you may inflict a child with my name. That child will wonder why, and ask, and so my memory will be kept green for a full generation."

"Longer than that," insisted Kim. "You'll never be forgotten here!"

Calhoun grinned at him.

Three days later, which was six days longer than he'd expected to be aground on Maris III, the landing grid heaved the little Med Ship out to space. The beautiful, nearly empty city dwindled as the grid field took the tiny spacecraft out to five planetary diameters and there released it. And Calhoun spun the Med Ship about and oriented it carefully for that place in the Cetis cluster where Med Service Headquarters was. He threw the overdrive switch.

The universe reeled. Calhoun's stomach seemed to turn over twice, and he had a sickish feeling of spiraling dizzily in what was somehow a cone. He swallowed. Murgatroyd made gulping noises. There was no longer a universe perceptible about the ship. There was dead silence. Then those small random noises began which have to be provided if a man is not to crack up in the dead stillness of a ship traveling at thirty times the speed of light.

Then there was nothing more to do. In overdrive travel there is never anything to do but pass the time away.

Murgatroyd took his right-hand whiskers in his right paw and licked them elaborately. He did the same to his left-hand whiskers. He contemplated the cabin, deciding upon a soft place in which to go to sleep.

"Murgatroyd," said Calhoun severely, "I have to have an argument with you. You imitate us humans too much! Kim Walpole caught you prowling around with an injector, starting

215

to give our prisoners another shot of polysulphate. It might have killed them! Personally, I think it would have been a good idea, but in a medical man it would have been most unethical. We professional men have to curb our impulses! Understand?"

"Chee!" said Murgatroyd. He curled up and wrapped his tail meticulously about his nose, preparing to doze.

Calhoun settled himself comfortably in his bunk. He picked up a book. It was Fitzgerald on *Probability and Human Conduct*.

He began to read as the ship went on through emptiness.

THE END